THE STORY THAT STARTED IT ALL!

"Damn, I hate this place!"

"*Ess?*" Jerry's head poked around the edge of the opening. "Who talking at, Davidge?"

I glared at the Drac, then waved my hand at it. "Nobody."

"*Ess va* 'nobody'?"

"Nobody. Nothing."

"*Ne gavey*, Davidge."

I poked at my chest with my finger. "Me! I'm talking to myself! You *gavey* that stuff, toadface!"

Jerry shook its head. "Davidge, now I sleep. Talk not so much nobody, *ne*?" It disappeared back into the opening.

"And so's your mother!" I turned and walked down the slope. *Except, strictly speaking, toadface, you don't have a mother—or father. "If you had your choice, who would you like to be trapped on a desert island with?"* I wondered if anyone ever picked a wet freezing corner of Hell shacked up with a hermaphrodite.

BARRY B.
LONGYEAR

ENEMY
MINE

AN AUTHORS GUILD BACKINPRINT.COM EDITION

Enemy Mine

AN AUTHORS GUILD BACKINPRINT.COM EDITION

Published by iUniverse, Inc.

For information address:
iUniverse, Inc.
2021 Pine Lake Road, Suite 100
Lincoln, NE 68512
www.iuniverse.com

Originally published by Tom Doherty Associates

This is a work of fiction. All the characters and events portrayed in
this book are fictitious, and any resemblance to real people or
events is purely coincidental.

ISBN: 0-595-30976-3

Printed in the United States of America

THE Dracon's three-fingered hands flexed. In the thing's yellow eyes I could read the desire to have those fingers around either a weapon or my throat. As I flexed my own fingers, I knew it read the same in my eyes.

"*Irkmaan!*" the thing spat.

"You piece of Drac slime." I brought my hands up in front of my chest and waved the thing on. "Come on, Drac; come and get it."

"*Irkmaan vaa, koruum su!*"

"Are you going to talk, or fight? Come on!" I could feel the spray from the sea behind me—a boiling madhouse of white-capped breakers that threatened to swallow me as it had my fighter. I had ridden my ship in. The Drac had ejected when its own fighter had caught one in the upper atmosphere, but not before crippling my power plant. I was exhausted from swimming to the grey, rocky beach and pulling myself to safety. Behind the Drac, among the rocks on the otherwise barren hill, I could see its ejection capsule. Far above us, its people and mine were still at it, slugging out the possession of an uninhabited corner of nowhere. The Drac just stood there and I went over the phrase taught us in training—a phrase calculated to drive any Drac into a frenzy. *"Kiz da yuomeen, Shizumaat!"* Meaning: Shizumaat, the most revered Drac philosopher, eats *kiz* excrement. Something on the level of stuffing a Moslem full of pork.

The Drac opened its mouth in horror, then closed it as anger literally changed its color from yellow to reddish-brown. *"Irkmaan, yaa stupid Mickey Mouse is!"*

I had taken an oath to fight and die over many things, but that venerable rodent didn't happen to be one of them. I laughed, and continued laughing until the guffaws in combination with my exhaustion forced me to my knees. I forced open my eyes to keep track of my enemy. The Drac was running toward the high ground, away from me and the sea. I half-turned toward the sea and caught a glimpse of a million tons of water just before they fell on me, knocking me unconscious.

"Kiz da yuomeen, Irkmaan, ne?"

My eyes were gritty with sand and stung with salt, but some part of my awareness pointed out: "Hey, you're alive." I reached to wipe the sand from my eyes and found my hands bound. A straight metal rod had been run through my sleeves and my wrists tied to it. As my tears cleared the sand from my eyes, I could see the Drac sitting on a smooth black boulder looking at me. It must have pulled me out of the drink. "Thanks, toadface. What's with the bondage?"

"Ess?"

I tried waving my arms and wound up giving an impression of an atmospheric fighter dipping its wings. "Untie me, you Drac slime!" I was seated on the sand, my back against a rock.

The Drac smiled, exposing the upper and lower mandibles that looked human—except that instead of separate teeth, they were solid. *"Eh, ne, Irkmaan."* It stood, walked over to me and checked my bonds.

"Untie me!"

The smile disappeared. *"Ne!"* It pointed at me with a yellow finger. *"Kos son va?"*

"I don't speak Drac, toadface. You speak Esper or English?"

The Drac delivered a very human-looking shrug, then pointed at its own chest. *"Kos va son Jeriba Shigan."* It pointed again at me. *"Kos son va?"*

"Davidge. My name is Willis E. Davidge."

"Ess?"

I tried my tongue on the unfamiliar syllables. *"Kos va son Willis Davidge."*

"Eh." Jeriba Shigan nodded, then motioned with its fingers. *"Dasu, Davidge."*

"Same to you, Jerry."

"Dasu, dasu!" Jeriba began sounding a little impatient. I shrugged as best I could. The Drac bent over and grabbed the front of my jumpsuit with both hands and pulled me to my feet. *"Dasu, dasu, kizlode!"*

"All right! So *dasu* is 'get up.' What's a *kizlode*?"

Jerry laughed. *"Gavey 'kiz'?"*

"Yeah, I *gavey*."

Jerry pointed at its head. *"Lode."* It pointed at my head. *"Kizlode, gavey?"*

I got it, then swung my arms around, catching Jerry upside its head with the metal rod. The Drac stumbled back against a rock, looking surprised. It raised a hand to its head and withdrew it covered with that pale pus that Dracs think is blood. It looked at me with murder in its eyes. *"Gefh! Nu Gefh*, Davidge!"

"Come and get it, Jerry, you *kizlode* sonofabitch!"

Jerry dived at me and I tried to catch it again with the rod, but the Drac caught my right wrist in both hands and, using the momentum of my swing, whirled me around, slamming my back against another rock. Just as I was getting back my breath, Jerry picked up a small boulder and came at me with every intention of turning my melon into pulp. With my back against the rock, I lifted a foot and kicked the Drac in the midsection, knocking it to the sand. I ran up, ready to stomp Jerry's melon, but he pointed behind me. I turned and saw another tidal wave gathering steam, and heading our way. *"Kiz!"* Jerry got to its feet and scampered for the high ground with me following close behind.

With the roar of the wave at our backs, we weaved among the water- and sand-ground black boulders until we reached Jerry's ejection capsule. The Drac stopped, put its shoulder to the egg-shaped contraption, and began rolling it uphill. I could see Jerry's point. The capsule contained all of the survival equipment and food either of us knew about. "Jerry!" I shouted above the rumble of the fast-approaching wave. "Pull out this damn rod and I'll help!" The Drac frowned at me. "The rod, *kizlode*, pull it out!" I cocked my head toward my outstretched arm.

Jerry placed a rock beneath the capsule to keep it from rolling back, then quickly untied my wrists and pulled out the rod. Both of us put our shoulders to the capsule, and we quickly rolled it to higher ground. The wave hit and climbed rapidly up the slope until it came up to our chests. The capsule bobbed like a cork, and it was all we could do to keep control of the thing until the water receded, wedging the capsule between three big boulders. I stood there, puffing.

Jerry dropped to the sand, its back against one of the boulders, and watched the water rush back out to sea. *"Magasienna!"*

"You said it, brother." I sank down next to the Drac; we agreed by eye to a temporary truce, and promptly passed out.

My eyes opened on a sky boiling with blacks and greys. Letting my head loll over on my left shoulder, I checked out the Drac. It was still out. First, I thought that this would be the perfect time to get the drop on Jerry. Second, I thought about how silly our insignificant scrap seemed compared to the insanity of the sea that surrounded us. Why hadn't the rescue team come? Did the Dracon fleet wipe us out? Why hadn't the Dracs come to pick up Jerry? Did they wipe out each other? I didn't even know where I was. An island. I had seen that much coming in, but where and in relation to what? Fyrine IV: the planet didn't even rate a name, but was important enough to die over.

With an effort, I struggled to my feet. Jerry opened its eyes and quickly pushed itself to a defensive crouching position. I waved my hand and shook my head. "Ease off, Jerry. I'm just going to look around." I turned my back on it and trudged off between the boulders. I walked uphill for a few minutes until I reached level ground.

It was an island, all right, and not a very big one. By eyeball estimation, height from sea level was only eighty meters, while the island itself was about two kilometers long and less than half that wide. The wind whipping my jumpsuit against my body was at least drying it out, but as I looked around at the smooth-ground boulders on top of the rise, I realized that Jerry and I could expect bigger waves than the few puny ones we had seen.

A rock clattered behind me and I turned to see Jerry climbing up the slope. When it reached the top, the Drac looked around. I squatted next to one of the boulders and passed my hand over it to indicate the smoothness, then I pointed toward the sea. Jerry nodded. *"Ae, gavey."* It pointed downhill toward the capsule, then to where we stood. *"Echey masu, nasesay."*

I frowned, then pointed at the capsule. *"Nasesay?* The capsule?"

"Ae, capsule *nasesay. Echey masu."* Jerry pointed at its feet.

I shook my head. "Jerry, if you *gavey* how these rocks got smooth"—I pointed at one—"then you *gavey* that *masu*ing the *nasesay* up here isn't going to do a damned bit of good." I made a sweeping up and down movement with my hands. "Waves." I pointed at the sea below. "Waves, up here." I pointed to where we stood. "Waves, *echey.*"

"Ae, gavey." Jerry looked around the top of the rise, then rubbed the side of its face. The Drac squatted next to some small rocks and began piling one on top of another. *"Viga,* Davidge."

I squatted next to it and watched while its nimble fingers constructed a circle of stones that quickly grew into a dollhouse-sized arena. Jerry stuck one of its fingers in the center of the circle. *"Echey, nasesay."*

The days on Fyrine IV seemed to be three times longer than any I had seen on any other habitable planet. I use the designation "habitable" with reservations. It took us most of the first day to painfully roll Jerry's *nasesay* up to the top of the rise. The night was too black to work and was bone-cracking cold. We removed the couch from the capsule, which made just enough room for both of us to fit inside. The body heat warmed things up a bit; and we killed time between sleeping, nibbling on Jerry's supply of ration bars (they taste a bit like fish mixed with cheddar cheese), and trying to come to some agreement about language.

"Eye."

"Thuyo."

"Finger."

"Zurath."

"Head."

The Drac laughed. *"Lode."*

"Ho, ho, very funny."

"Ho, ho."

At dawn on the second day, we rolled and pushed the capsule into the center of the rise and wedged it between two large rocks, one of which had an overhang that we hoped would hold down the capsule when one of those big soakers hit. Around the rocks and capsule, we laid a foundation of large stones and filled in the cracks with smaller stones. By the time the wall was knee high, we discovered that building with those smooth, round stones and no mortar wasn't going to work. After some experimentation, we figured out how to break the stones to give us flat sides with which to work. It's done by picking up one stone and slamming it down on top of another. We took turns, one slamming and one building. The stone was almost a volcanic glass, and we also took turns extracting rock splinters from each other. It took nine of those endless days and nights to complete the walls, during which waves came close many times and once washed us ankle deep. For six of those nine days, it rained. The capsule's survival equipment included a plastic blanket, and that became our roof. It sagged in at the center, and the hole we put in it there allowed the water to run out, keeping us almost dry and giving us a supply of fresh water. If a wave of any determination came along, we could kiss the roof goodbye; but we both had confidence in the walls, which were almost two meters thick at the bottom and at least a meter thick at the top.

After we finished, we sat inside and admired our work for about an hour, until it dawned on us that we had just worked ourselves out of jobs. "What now, Jerry?"

"*Ess?*"

"What do we do now?"

"Now wait, we." The Drac shrugged. "Else what, *ne?*"

I nodded. "*Gavey.*" I got to my feet and walked to the passageway we had built. With no wood for a door, where the walls would have met, we bent one out and extended it about three meters around the other wall with the opening away from the prevailing winds. The never-ending winds were still at it, but the rain had stopped. The shack wasn't much to look at, but looking at it stuck there in the center of that deserted island made me feel good. As Shizumaat observed, "Intelligent life making its stand against the universe." Or, at least, that's the sense I could make out of Jerry's hamburger of English. I shrugged and picked up a sharp splinter of stone and made another mark in the large standing rock that served as my log. Ten scratches in all, and under the seventh, a small x to indicate the big wave that just covered the top of the island.

I threw down the splinter. "Damn, I hate this place!"

"*Ess?*" Jerry's head poked around the edge of the opening. "Who talking at, Davidge?"

I glared at the Drac, then waved my hand at it. "Nobody."

"*Ess va* 'nobody'?"

"Nobody. Nothing."

"*Ne gavey*, Davidge."

I poked at my chest with my finger. "Me! I'm talking to myself! You *gavey* that stuff, toadface!"

Jerry shook its head. "Davidge, now I sleep. Talk not so much nobody, *ne?*" It disappeared back into the opening.

"And so's your mother!" I turned and walked down the slope. *Except, strictly speaking, toadface, you don't have a mother—or father. "If you had your choice, who would you like to be trapped on a desert island with?"* I wondered if anyone ever picked a wet freezing corner of Hell shacked up with a hermaphrodite.

Half of the way down the slope, I followed the path I had marked with rocks until I came to my

tidal pool that I had named "Rancho Sluggo."
Around the pool were many of the water-worn
rocks, and underneath those rocks, below the
pool's waterline, lived the fattest orange slugs
either of us had ever seen. I made the discovery
during a break from house building and showed
them to Jerry.

Jerry shrugged. "And so?"

"And so what? Look, Jerry, those ration bars
aren't going to last forever. What are we going to
eat when they're all gone?"

"Eat?" Jerry looked at the wriggling pocket of
insect life and grimaced. "*Ne*, Davidge. Before then
pickup. Search us find, then pickup."

"What if they don't find us? What then?"

Jerry grimaced again and turned back to the
half-completed house. "Water we drink, then until
pickup." He had muttered something about *kiz*
excrement and my tastebuds, then walked out of
sight.

Since then I had built up the pool's walls, hoping
the increased protection from the harsh environ-
ment would increase the herd. I looked under
several rocks, but no increase was apparent. And,
again, I couldn't bring myself to swallow one of the
things. I replaced the rock I was looking under,
stood and looked out to the sea. Although the eternal cloud cover still denied the surface the drying rays of Fyrine, there was no rain and the
usual haze had lifted.

In the direction past where I had pulled myself
up on the beach, the sea continued to the horizon.
In the spaces between the whitecaps, the water was
as grey as a loan officer's heart. Parallel lines of
rollers formed approximately five kilometers from
the island. The center, from where I was standing,

would smash on the island, while the remainder steamed on. To my right, in line with the breakers, I could just make out another small island perhaps ten kilometers away. Following the path of the rollers, I looked far to my right, and where the grey-white of the sea should have met the lighter grey of the sky, there was a black line on the horizon.

The harder I tried to remember the briefing charts on Fyrine IV's land masses, the less clear it became. Jerry couldn't remember anything either —at least nothing it would tell me. Why should we remember? The battle was supposed to be in space, each one trying to deny the other an orbital staging area in the Fyrine system. Neither side wanted to set foot on Fyrine, much less fight a battle there. Still, whatever it was called, it was land and considerably larger than the sand and rock bar we were occupying.

How to get there was the problem. Without wood, fire, leaves, or animal skins, Jerry and I were destitute compared to the average poverty-stricken caveman. The only thing we had that would float was the *nasesay*. The capsule. Why not? The only real problem to overcome was getting Jerry to go along with it.

That evening, while the greyness made its slow transition to black, Jerry and I sat outside the shack nibbling our quarter portions of ration bars. The Drac's yellow eyes studied the dark line on the horizon, then it shook its head. "*Ne*, Davidge. Dangerous is."

I popped the rest of my ration bar into my mouth and talked around it. "Any more dangerous than staying here?"

"Soon pickup, *ne*?"

I studied those yellow eyes. "Jerry, you don't believe that any more than I do." I leaned forward on the rock and held out my hands. "Look, our chances will be a lot better on a larger land mass. Protection from the big waves, maybe food . . ."

"Not maybe, *ne?*" Jerry pointed at the water. "How *nasesay* steer, Davidge? In that, how steer? *Ess eh* soakers, waves, beyond land take, *gavey? Bresha*," Jerry's hands slapped together. *"Ess eh bresha* rocks on, *ne?* Then we death."

I scratched my head. "The waves are going in that direction from here, and so is the wind. If the land mass is large enough, we don't have to steer, *gavey?*"

Jerry snorted. *"Ne* large enough, then?"

"I didn't say it was a sure thing."

"Ess?"

"A sure thing; certain, *gavey?*" Jerry nodded. "And for smashing up on the rocks, it probably has a beach like this one."

"Sure thing, *ne?*"

I shrugged. "No, it's not a sure thing, but, what about staying here? We don't know how big those waves can get. What if one just comes along and washes us off the island? What then?"

Jerry looked at me, its eyes narrowed. "What there, Davidge? *Irkmaan* base, *ne?*"

I laughed. "I told you, we don't have any bases on Fyrine IV."

"Why want go, then?"

"Just what I said, Jerry. I think our chances would be better."

"Ummm." The Drac folded its arms. *"Viga,* Davidge, *nasesay* stay. I know."

"Know what?"

Jerry smirked, then stood and went into the shack. After a moment it returned and threw a two-meter long metal rod at my feet. It was the one the Drac had used to bind my arms. "Davidge, I know."

I raised my eyebrows and shrugged. "What are you talking about? Didn't that come from your capsule?"

"*Ne, Irkmaan.*"

I bent down and picked up the rod. Its surface was uncorroded and at one end were arabic numerals—a part number. For a moment a flood of hope washed over me, but it drained away when I realized it was a civilian part number. I threw the rod on the sand. "There's no telling how long that's been here, Jerry. It's a civilian part number and no civilian missions have been in this part of the galaxy since the war. Might be left over from an old seeding operation or exploratory mission . . ."

The Drac nudged it with the toe of his boot. "New, *gavey?*"

I looked up at it. "You *gavey* stainless steel?"

Jerry snorted and turned back toward the shack. "I stay, *nasesay* stay; where you want, you go, Davidge!"

With the black of the long night firmly bolted down on us, the wind picked up, shrieking and whistling in and through the holes in the walls. The plastic roof flapped, pushed in and sucked out with such violence it threatened to either tear or sail off into the night. Jerry sat on the sand floor, its back leaning against the *nasesay* as if to make clear that both Drac and capsule were staying put, although the way the sea was picking up seemed to weaken Jerry's argument.

"Sea rough now is, Davidge, *ne*?"

"It's too dark to see, but with this wind . . ." I shrugged more for my own benefit than the Drac's, since the only thing visible inside the shack was the pale light coming through the roof. Any minute we could be washed off that sandbar. "Jerry, you're being silly about that rod. You know that."

"*Surda*." The Drac sounded contrite if not altogether miserable.

"*Ess*?"

"*Ess eh 'surda'*?"

"*Ae*."

Jerry remained silent for a moment. "Davidge, *gavey* 'not certain not is'?"

I sorted out the negatives. "You mean 'possible,' 'maybe,' 'perhaps'?"

"*Ae*, possiblemaybeperhaps. Dracon fleet *Irkmaan* ships have. Before war buy; after war capture. Rod possiblemaybeperhaps Dracon is."

"So, if there's a secret base on the big island, *surda* it's a Dracon base?"

"Possiblemaybeperhaps, Davidge."

"Jerry, does that mean you want to try it? The *nasesay*?"

"*Ne*."

"*Ne*? Why, Jerry? If it might be a Drac base—"

"*Ne*! *Ne* talk!" The Drac seemed to choke on the words.

"Jerry, we talk, and you better *believe* we talk! If I'm going to death it on this island, I have a right to know why."

The Drac was quiet for a long time. "Davidge."

"*Ess*?"

"*Nasesay* you take. Half ration bars you leave. I stay."

I shook my head to clear it. "You want me to take the capsule alone?"

"What you want is, *ne?*"

"*Ae*, but why? You must realize there won't be any pickup."

"Possiblemaybeperhaps."

"*Surda*, nothing. You know there isn't going to be a pickup. What is it? You afraid of the water? If that's it, we have a better chance—"

"Davidge, up your mouth shut. *Nasesay* you have. Me *ne* you need, *gavey?*"

I nodded in the dark. The capsule was mine for the taking; what did I need a grumpy Drac along for—especially since our truce could expire at any moment? The answer made me feel a little silly—human. Perhaps it's the same thing. The Drac was all that stood between me and utter aloneness. Still, there was the small matter of staying alive. "We should go together, Jerry."

"Why?"

I felt myself blush. If humans have this need for companionship, why are they also ashamed to admit it? "We just should. Our chances would be better."

"Alone your chances better are, Davidge. Your enemy I am."

I nodded again and grimaced in the dark. "Jerry, you *gavey* 'loneliness'?"

"*Ne gavey.*"

"Lonely. Being alone, by myself."

"*Gavey* you alone. Take *nasesay*; I stay."

"That's it . . . see, *viga*, I don't want to."

"You want together go?" A low, dirty chuckle came from the other side of the shack. "You

Dracon like? You me death, *Irkmaan*." Jerry chuckled some more. "*Irkmaan poorzhab* in head, *poorzhab*."

"Forget it!" I slid down from the wall, smoothed out the sand, and curled up with my back toward the Drac. The wind seemed to die down a bit and I closed my eyes to try and sleep. In a bit, the snap, crack of the plastic roof blended in with the background of shrieks and whistles and I felt myself drifting off, when my eyes opened wide at the sound of footsteps in the sand. I tensed, ready to spring.

"Davidge?" Jerry's voice was very quiet.

"What?"

I heard the Drac sit on the sand next to me. "You loneliness, Davidge. About it hard you talk, *ne*?"

"So what?" The Drac mumbled something that was lost in the wind. "What?" I turned over and saw Jerry looking through a hole in the wall.

"Why I stay. Now, you I tell, *ne*?"

I shrugged. "Okay; why not?"

Jerry seemed to struggle with the words, then opened its mouth to speak. Its eyes opened wide. "*Magasienna!*"

I sat up. "*Ess?*"

Jerry pointed at the hole. "Soaker!"

I pushed it out of the way and looked through the hole. Steaming toward our island was an insane mountainous fury of white-capped rollers. It was hard to tell in the dark, but the one in front looked taller than the one that had wet our feet a few days before. The ones following it were bigger. Jerry put a hand on my shoulder and I looked into the Drac's eyes. We broke and ran for the capsule. We heard the first wave rumbling up the slope as we felt around in the dark for the recessed doorlatch. I just got my finger on it when the wave smashed against the shack, collapsing the roof. In half a second we were underwater, the currents inside the shack agitating us like socks in a washing machine.

The water receded, and as I cleared my eyes, I saw that the windward wall of the shack had caved in. "Jerry!"

Through the collapsed wall, I saw the Drac staggering around outside. *"Irkmaan?"* Behind him I could see the second roller gathering speed.

"Kizlode, what'n the Hell you doing out there? Get in here!"

I turned to the capsule, still lodged firmly between the two rocks, and found the handle. As I opened the door, Jerry stumbled through the missing wall and fell against me. "Davidge . . . forever soakers go on! Forever!"

"Get in!" I helped the Drac through the door and didn't wait for it to get out of the way. I piled in on top of Jerry and latched the door just as the second wave hit. I could feel the capsule lift a bit and rattle against the overhang of the one rock.

"Davidge, we float?"

"No. The rocks are holding us. We'll be all right once the breakers stop."

"Over you move."

"Oh." I got off Jerry's chest and braced myself against one end of the capsule. After a bit, the capsule came to rest and we waited for the next one. "Jerry?"

"Ess?"

"What was it that you were about to say?"

"Why I stay?"

"Yeah."

"About it hard me talk, *gavey?"*

"I know, I know."

The next breaker hit and I could feel the capsule rise and rattle against the rock. "Davidge, *gavey 'vi nessa'*?"

"*Ne gavey.*"

"*Vi nessa* . . . little me, *gavey*?"

The capsule bumped down the rock and came to rest. "What about little you?"

"Little me . . . little Drac. From me, *gavey*?"

"Are you telling me you're *pregnant*?"

"Possiblemaybeperhaps."

I shook my head. "Hold on, Jerry. I don't want any misunderstandings. Pregnant . . . are you going to be a parent?"

"*Ae*, parent, two-zero-zero in line, very important is, *ne*?"

"Terrific. What's this got to do with you not wanting to go to the other island?"

"Before, me *vi nessa, gavey? Tean* death."

"Your child, it died?"

"*Ae!*" The Drac's sob was torn from the lips of the universal mother. "I in fall hurt. *Tean* death. *Nasesay* in sea us bang. *Tean* hurt, *gavey*?"

"*Ae*, I *gavey*." So Jerry was afraid of losing another child. It was almost certain that the capsule trip would bang us around a lot, but staying on the sandbar didn't appear to be improving our chances. The capsule had been at rest for quite a while, and I decided to risk a peek outside. The small canopy windows seemed to be covered with sand, and I opened the door. I looked around, and all of the walls had been smashed flat. I looked toward the sea, but could see nothing. "It looks safe, Jerry . . ." I looked up, toward the blackish sky, and above me towered the white plume of a

descending breaker. *"Maga* damn *sienna!"* I
slammed the hatch door.
   "Ess, Davidge?"
   "Hang on, Jerry!"
The sound of the water hitting the capsule was
beyond hearing. We banged once, twice against the
rock, then we could feel ourselves twisting, shoot-
ing upward. I made a grab to hang on, but missed
as the capsule took a sickening lurch downward. I
fell into Jerry, then was flung to the opposite wall,
where I struck my head. Before I went blank, I
heard Jerry cry *"Tean! Vi tean!"*

   . . . *the lieutenant pressed his hand control and a
figure—tall, humanoid, yellow—appeared on the
screen.*
   *"Dracslime!" shouted the auditorium of seated
recruits.*
   *The lieutenant faced the recruits. "Correct. This is
a Drac. Note that the Drac race is uniform as to color;
they are all yellow." The recruits chuckled politely.
The officer preened a bit, then with a light wand
began pointing out various features. "The three-
fingered hands are distinctive, of course, as is the
almost noseless face, which gives the Drac a toadlike
appearance. On average, eyesight is slightly better
than human, hearing about the same, and smell . . ."
The lieutenant paused. "The smell is terrible!" The
officer beamed at the uproar from the recruits. When
the auditorium quieted down, he pointed his light
wand at a fold in the figure's belly. "This is where the
Drac keeps its family jewels—all of them." Another
chuckle. "That's right, Dracs are hermaphrodites,*

with both male and female reproductive organs contained in the same individual." The lieutenant faced the recruits. "You go tell a Drac to go boff himself, then watch out, because he can!" The laughter died down, and the lieutenant held out a hand toward the screen. "You see one of these things, what do you do?"

"KILL IT . . ."

. . . I cleared the screen and computer sighted on the next Drac fighter, looking like a double x in the screen's display. The Drac shifted hard to the left, then right again. I felt the autopilot pull my ship after the fighter, sorting out and ignoring the false images, trying to lock its electronic crosshairs on the Drac. "Come on, toadface . . . a little bit to the left . . ." The double cross image moved into the ranging rings on the display and I felt the missle attached to the belly of my fighter take off. "Gotcha!" Through my canopy I saw the flash as the missile detonated. My screen showed the Drac fighter out of control, spinning toward Fyrine IV's cloud-shrouded surface. I dived after it to confirm the kill . . . skin temperature increasing as my ship brushed the upper atmosphere. "Come on, dammit, blow!" I shifted the ship's systems over for atmospheric flight when it became obvious that I'd have to follow the Drac right to the ground. Still above the clouds, the Drac stopped spinning and turned. I hit the auto override and pulled the stick into my lap. The fighter wallowed as it tried to pull up. Everyone knows the Drac ships work better in atmosphere . . . heading toward me on an interception course . . . why doesn't the slime fire? . . . just before the collision, the Drac ejects . . .

power gone; have to deadstick it in. I track the
capsule as it falls through the muck, intending to find
that Dracslime and finish the job. . . .

It could have been for seconds or years that I
groped into the darkness around me. I felt touch-
ing, but the parts of me being touched seemed far,
far away. First chills, then fever, then chills again,
my head being cooled by a gentle hand. I opened
my eyes to narrow slits and saw Jerry hovering over
me, blotting my forehead with something cool. I
managed a whisper. "Jerry."

The Drac looked into my eyes and smiled. "Good
is, Davidge. Good is."

The light on Jerry's face flickered and I smelled
smoke. "Fire."

Jerry got out of the way and pointed toward the
center of the room's sandy floor. I let my head roll
over and realized that I was lying on a bed of soft,
springy branches. Opposite my bed was another
bed, and between them crackled a cheery campfire. "Fire now we have, Davidge. And wood." Jerry
pointed toward the roof made of wooden poles
thatched with broad leaves.

I turned and looked around, then let my throb-
bing head sink down and closed my eyes. "Where
are we?"

"Big island, Davidge. Soaker off sandbar us
washed. Wind and waves us here took. Right you
were."

"I . . . I don't understand; *ne gavey*. It'd take days
to get to the big island from the sandbar."

Jerry nodded and dropped what looked like a
sponge into a shell of some sort filled with water.

"Nine days. You I strap to *nasesay*, then here on beach we land."

"Nine days? I've been out for nine days?"

Jerry shook his head. "Seventeen. Here we land eight days . . ." The Drac waved its hand behind itself.

"Ago . . . eight days ago."

"*Ae.*"

Seventeen days on Fyrine IV was better than a month on Earth. I opened my eyes again and looked at Jerry. The Drac was almost bubbling with excitement. "What about your *tean*, your child?"

Jerry patted its swollen middle. "Good is, Davidge. You more *nasesay* hurt."

I overcame an urge to nod. "I'm happy for you." I closed my eyes and turned my face toward the wall, a combination of wood poles and leaves. "Jerry?"

"*Ess?*"

"You saved my life."

"*Ae.*"

"Why?"

Jerry sat quietly for a long time. "Davidge. On sandbar you talk. Loneliness now *gavey*." The Drac shook my arm. "Here, now you eat."

I turned and looked into a shell filled with a steaming liquid. "What is it, chicken soup?"

"*Ess?*"

"*Ess va?*" I pointed at the bowl, realizing for the first time how weak I was.

Jerry frowned. "Like slug, but long."

"An eel?"

"*Ae*, but eel on land, *gavey*?"

"You mean 'snake'?"

"Possiblemaybeperhaps."

I nodded and put my lips to the edge of the shell. I sipped some of the broth, swallowed and let the broth's healing warmth seep through my body. "Good."

"You *custa* want?"

"*Ess?*"

"*Custa.*" Jerry reached next to the fire and picked up a squareish chunk of clear rock. I looked at it, scratched it with my thumbnail, then touched it with my tongue.

"Halite! Salt!"

Jerry smiled. "*Custa* you want?"

I laughed. "All the comforts. By all means, let's have *custa.*"

Jerry took the halite, knocked off a corner with a small stone, then used the stone to grind the pieces against another stone. He held out the palm of his hand with a tiny mountain of white granules in the center. I took two pinches, dropped them into my snake soup and stirred it with my finger. Then I took a long swallow of the delicious broth. I smacked my lips. "Fantastic."

"Good, *ne?*"

"Better than good; fantastic." I took another swallow, making a big show of smacking my lips and rolling my eyes.

"Fantastic, Davidge, *ne?*"

"*Ae.*" I nodded at the Drac. "I think that's enough. I want to sleep."

"*Ae*, Davidge, *gavey.*" Jerry took the bowl and put it beside the fire. The Drac stood, walked to the door and turned back. Its yellow eyes studied me for an instant, then it nodded, turned and went outside. I closed my eyes and let the heat from the campfire coax the sleep over me.

* * *

In two days I was up in the shack trying my legs, and in two more days Jerry helped me outside. The shack was located at the top of a long gentle rise in a scrub forest; none of the trees was any taller than five or six meters. At the bottom of the slope, better than eight kilometers from the shack, was the still-rolling sea. The Drac had carried me. Our trusty *nasesay* had filled with water and had been dragged back into the sea soon after Jerry pulled me to dry land. With it went the remainder of the ration bars. Dracs are very fussy about what they eat, but hunger finally drove Jerry to sample some of the local flora and fauna—hunger and the human lump that was rapidly drifting away from lack of nourishment. The Drac had settled on a bland, starchy type of root, a green bushberry that when dried made an acceptable tea, and snakemeat. Exploring, Jerry had found a partly eroded salt dome. In the days that followed, I grew stronger and added to our diet with several types of sea mollusk and a fruit resembling a cross between a pear and a plum.

As the days grew colder, the Drac and I were forced to realize that Fyrine IV had a winter. Given that, we had to face the possibility that the winter would be severe enough to prevent the gathering of food—and wood. When dried next to the fire, the berrybush and roots kept well, and we tried both salting and smoking snakemeat. With strips of fiber from the berrybush for thread, Jerry and I pieced together the snakeskins for winter clothing. The design we settled on involved two layers of skins with the down from berrybush seed pods stuffed between and then held in place by quilting the layers.

We agreed that the house would never do. It took

three days of searching to find our first cave, and another three days before we found one that suited us. The mouth opened onto a view of the eternally tormented sea, but was set in the face of a low cliff well above sea level. Around the cave's entrance we found great quantities of dead wood and loose stone. The wood we gathered for heat; and the stone we used to wall up the entrance, leaving only space enough for a hinged door. The hinges were made of snake leather and the door of wooden poles tied together with berrybush fiber. The first night after completing the door, the sea winds blew it to pieces; and we decided to go back to the original door design we had used on the sandbar.

Deep inside the cave, we made our living quarters in a chamber with a wide, sandy floor. Still deeper, the cave had natural pools of water, which were fine for drinking but too cold for bathing. We used the pool chamber for our supply room. We lined the walls of our living quarters with piles of wood and made new beds out of snakeskins and seed pod down. In the center of the chamber we built a respectable fireplace with a large, flat stone over the coals for a griddle. The first night we spent in our new home, I discovered that, for the first time since ditching on that damned planet, I couldn't hear the wind.

During the long nights, we would sit at the fireplace making things—gloves, hats, packbags—out of snake leather, and we would talk. To break the monotony, we alternated days between speaking Drac and English, and by the time the winter hit with its first ice storm, each of us was comfortable in the other's language.

We talked of Jerry's coming child.

"What are you going to name it, Jerry?"

"It already has a name. See, the Jeriba line has five names. My name is Shigan; before me came my parent, Gothig; before Gothig was Haesni; before Haesni was Ty, and before Ty was Zammis. The child is named Jeriba Zammis."

"Why only the five names? A human child can have just about any name its parents pick for it. In fact, once a human becomes an adult, he or she can pick any name he or she wants."

The Drac looked at me, its eyes filled with pity. "Davidge, how lost you must feel. You humans— how lost you must feel."

"Lost?"

Jerry nodded. "Where do you come from, Davidge?"

"You mean my parents?"

"Yes."

I shrugged. "I remember my parents."

"And their parents?"

"I remember my mother's father. When I was young we used to visit him."

"Davidge, what do you know about this grandparent?"

I rubbed my chin. "It's kind of vague . . . I think he was in some kind of agriculture—I don't know."

"And his parents?"

I shook my head. "The only thing I remember is that somewhere along the line, English and Germans figured. *Gavey* Germans and English?"

Jerry nodded. "Davidge, I can recite the history of my line back to the founding of my planet by Jeriba Ty, one of the original settlers, one hundred and ninety-nine generations ago. At our line's archives on Draco, there are the records that trace the line across space to the racehome planet, Sindie, and there back seventy generations to Jeriba Ty, the founder of the Jeriba line."

"How does one become a founder?"

"Only the firstborn carries the line. Products of second, third, or fourth births must found their own lines."

I nodded, impressed. "Why only the five names? Just to make it easier to remember them?"

Jerry shook its head. "No. The names are things to which we add distinction; they are the same, commonplace five so that they do not overshadow the events that distinguish their bearers. The name I carry, Shigan, has been served by great soldiers, scholars, students of philosophy, and several priests. The name my child will carry has been served by scientists, teachers, and explorers."

"You remember all of your ancestors' occupations?"

Jerry nodded. "Yes, and what they each did and where they did it. You must recite your line before the line's archives to be admitted into adulthood as I was twenty-two of my years ago. Zammis will do the same, except the child must begin its recitation"—Jerry smiled—"with my name, Jeriba Shigan."

"You can recite almost two hundred biographies from memory?"

"Yes."

I went over to my bed and stretched out. As I stared up at the smoke being sucked through the crack in the chamber's ceiling, I began to understand what Jerry meant by feeling lost. A Drac with several dozens of generations under its belt knew who it was and what it had to live up to. "Jerry?"

"Yes, Davidge?"

"Will you recite them for me?" I turned my head and looked at the Drac in time to see an expression of utter surprise melt into joy. It was only after many years had passed that I learned I had done Jerry a great honor in requesting his line. Among the Dracs, it is a rare expression of respect, not only of the individual, but of the line.

Jerry placed the hat he was sewing on the sand, stood and began.

"Before you here I stand, Shigan of the line of Jeriba, born of Gothig, the teacher of music. A musician of high merit, the students of Gothig include Datzizh of the Nem line, Perravane of the Tuscor line, and many lesser musicians. Trained in music at the Shimuram, Gothig stood before the archives in the year 11,051 and spoke of its parent Haesni, the manufacturer of ships . . ."

As I listened to Jerry's singsong of formal Dracon, the backward biographies—beginning with death and ending with adulthood—I experienced a sense of time-binding, of being able to know and touch the past. Battles, empires built and destroyed, discoveries made, great things done—a tour through twelve thousand years of history, but perceived as a well-defined, living continuum.

Against this: I, Willis of the Davidge line, stand before you, born of Sybil the housewife and Nathan the second-rate civil engineer, one of them born of Grandpop, who probably had something to do with agriculture, born of nobody in particular. . . . Hell, I wasn't even that! My older brother carried the line; not me. I listened and made up my mind to memorize the line of Jeriba.

* * *

We talked of war:

"That was a pretty neat trick, suckering me into the atmosphere, then ramming me."

Jerry shrugged. "Dracon fleet pilots are best; this is well known."

I raised my eyebrows. "That's why I shot your tail feathers off, huh?"

Jerry shrugged, frowned, and continued sewing on the scraps of snake leather. "Why do the Earthmen invade this part of the galaxy, Davidge? We had thousands of years of peace before you came."

"Hah! Why do the Dracs invade? We were at peace too. What are you doing here?"

"We settle these planets. It is the Drac tradition. We are explorers and founders."

"Well, toadface, what do you think we are, a bunch of homebodies? Humans have had space travel for less than two hundred years, but we've settled almost twice as many planets as the Dracs—"

Jerry held up a finger. "Exactly! You humans spread like a disease. Enough! We don't want you here!"

"Well, we're here, and here to stay. Now what are you going to do about it?"

"You see what we do, *Irkmaan*, we fight!"

"Phooey! You call that little scrap we were in a fight? Hell, Jerry, we were kicking you junk jocks out of the sky—"

"Haw, Davidge! That's why you sit here sucking on smoked snakemeat!"

I pulled the little rascal out of my mouth and pointed it at the Drac. "I notice your breath has a snake flavor too, Drac!"

Jerry snorted and turned away from the fire. I felt stupid, first because we weren't going to settle

an argument that had plagued a hundred worlds
for over a century. Second, I wanted to have Jerry
check my recitation. I had over a hundred generations memorized. The Drac's side was toward the
fire, leaving enough light falling on its lap to see its
sewing.

"Jerry, what are you working on?"

"We have nothing to talk about, Davidge."

"Come on, what is it?"

Jerry turned its head toward me, then looked
back into its lap and picked up a tiny snakeskin
suit. "For Zammis." Jerry smiled and I shook my
head, then laughed.

We talked of philosophy:

"You studied Shizumaat, Jerry; why won't you
tell me about its teachings?"

Jerry frowned. "No, Davidge."

"Are Shizumaat's teachings secret or something?"

Jerry shook its head. "No. But we honor
Shizumaat too much for talk."

I rubbed my chin. "Do you mean too much to
talk about it, or to talk about it with a human?"

"Not with humans, Davidge; just not with you."

"Why?"

Jerry lifted its head and narrowed its yellow eyes.
"You know what you said . . . on the sandbar."

I scratched my head and vaguely recalled the
curse I laid on the Drac about Shizumaat eating it.
I held out my hands. "But, Jerry, I was mad, angry.
You can't hold me accountable for what I said
then."

"I do."

"Will it change anything if I apologize?"

"Not a thing."

I stopped myself from saying something nasty and thought back to that moment when Jerry and I stood ready to strangle each other. I remembered something about that meeting and screwed the corners of my mouth in place to keep from smiling. "Will you tell me Shizumaat's teachings if I forgive you . . . for what you said about Mickey Mouse?" I bowed my head in an appearance of reverence, although its chief purpose was to suppress a cackle.

Jerry looked up at me, its face pained with guilt. "I have felt bad about that, Davidge. If you forgive me, I will talk about Shizumaat."

"Then I forgive you, Jerry."

"One more thing."

"What?"

"You must tell me of the teachings of Mickey Mouse."

"I'll . . . uh, do my best."

We talked of Zammis:

"Jerry, what do you want little Zammy to be?"

The Drac shrugged. "Zammis must live up to its own name. I want it to do that with honor. If Zammis does that, it is all I can ask."

"Zammy will pick its own trade?"

"Yes."

"Isn't there anything special you want, though?"

Jerry nodded. "Yes, there is."

"What's that?"

"That Zammis will, one day, find itself off this miserable planet."

I nodded. "Amen."

"Amen."

The winter dragged on until Jerry and I began wondering if we had gotten in on the beginning of an ice age. Outside the cave, everything was coated with a thick layer of ice, and the low temperature combined with the steady winds made venturing outside a temptation of death by falls or freezing. Still, by mutual agreement, we both went outside to relieve ourselves. There were several isolated chambers deep in the cave; but we feared polluting our water supply, not to mention the air inside the cave. The main risk outside was dropping one's drawers at a wind chill factor that froze breath vapor before it could be blown through the thin face muffs we had made out of our flight suits. We learned not to dawdle.

One morning, Jerry was outside answering the call, while I stayed by the fire mashing up dried roots with water for griddle cakes. I heard Jerry call from the mouth of the cave. "Davidge!"

"What?"

"Davidge, come quick!"

A ship! It had to be! I put the shell bowl on the sand, put on my hat and gloves, and ran through the passage. As I came close to the door, I untied the muff from around my neck and tied it over my mouth and nose to protect my lungs. Jerry, its head bundled in a similar manner, was looking through the door, waving me on. "What is it?"

Jerry stepped away from the door to let me through. "Come, look!"

Sunlight. Blue sky and sunlight. In the distance, over the sea, new clouds were piling up; but above us the sky was clear. Neither of us could look at the sun directly, but we turned our faces to it and felt the rays of Fyrine on our skins. The light glared and sparkled off the ice-covered rocks and trees. "Beautiful."

"Yes." Jerry grabbed my sleeve with a gloved hand. "Davidge, you know what this means?"

"What?"

"Signal fires at night. On a clear night, a large fire could be seen from orbit, *ne?*"

I looked at Jerry, then back at the sky. "I don't know. If the fire were big enough, and we get a clear night, and if anybody picks that moment to look . . ." I let my head hang down. "That's always supposing that there's someone in orbit up there to do the looking." I felt the pain begin in my fingers. "We better go back in."

"Davidge, it's a chance!"

"What are we going to use for wood, Jerry?" I held out an arm toward the trees above and around the cave. "Everything that can burn has at least fifteen centimeters of ice on it."

"In the cave—"

"Our firewood?" I shook my head. "How long is this winter going to last? Can you be sure that we have enough wood to waste on signal fires?"

"It's a chance, Davidge. It's a chance!"

Our survival riding on a toss of the dice. I shrugged. "Why not?"

We spent the next few hours hauling a quarter of our carefully gathered firewood and dumping it outside the mouth of the cave. By the time we were finished and long before night came, the sky was again a solid blanket of grey. Several times each night, we would check the sky, waiting for stars to appear. During the days, we would frequently have to spend several hours beating the ice off the wood pile. Still, it gave both of us hope, until the wood in the cave ran out and we had to start borrowing from the signal pile.

That night, for the first time, the Drac looked absolutely defeated. Jerry sat at the fireplace, staring at the flames. Its hand reached inside its snakeskin jacket through the neck and pulled out a small golden cube suspended on a chain. Jerry held the cube clasped in both hands, shut its eyes, and began mumbling in Drac. I watched from my bed until Jerry finished. The Drac sighed, nodded, and replaced the object within its jacket.

"What's that thing?"

Jerry looked up at me, frowned, then touched the front of its jacket. "This? It is my *Talman*—what you call a Bible."

"A Bible is a book. You know, with pages that you read."

Jerry pulled the thing from its jacket, mumbled a phrase in Drac, then worked a small catch. Another gold cube dropped from the first and the Drac held it out to me. "Be very careful with it, Davidge."

I sat up, took the object, and examined it in the light of the fire. Three hinged pieces of the golden metal formed the binding of a book two-and-a-half centimeters on an edge. I opened the book in the middle and looked over the double columns of dots, lines, and squiggles. "It's in Drac."

"Of course."

"But I can't read it."

Jerry's eyebrows went up. "You speak Drac so well, I didn't remember . . . would you like me to teach you?"

"To read this?"

"Why not? You have an appointment you have to keep?"

I shrugged. "No." I touched my finger to the book and tried to turn one of the tiny pages. Perhaps fifty pages went at once. "I can't separate the pages."

Jerry pointed at a small bump at the top of the spine. "Pull out the pin. It's for turning the pages."

I pulled out the short needle, touched it against a page, and it slid loose of its companion and flipped. "Who wrote your *Talman*, Jerry?"

"Many. All great teachers."

"Shizumaat?"

Jerry nodded. "Shizumaat is one of them."

I closed the book and held it in the palm of my hand. "Jerry, why did you bring this out now?"

"I needed its comfort." The Drac held out its arms. "This place. Maybe we will grow old here and die. Maybe we will never be found. I see this today as we brought in the signal fire wood." Jerry placed its hands on its belly. "Zammis will be born here. The *Talman* helps me to accept what I cannot change."

"Zammis, how much longer?"

Jerry smiled. "Soon."

I looked at the tiny book. "I would like you to teach me to read this, Jerry."

The Drac took the chain and case from around its neck and handed it to me. "You must keep the *Talman* in this."

I held it for a moment, then shook my head. "I can't keep this, Jerry. It's obviously of great value to you. What if I lost it?"

"You won't. Keep it while you learn. The student must do this."

I put the chain around my neck. "This is quite an honor you do me."

Jerry shrugged. "Much less than the honor you

do me by memorizing the Jeriba line. Your recitations have been accurate, and moving." Jerry took some charcoal from the fire, stood, and walked to the wall of the chamber. That night I learned the thirty-one letters and sounds of the Drac alphabet, as well as the additional nine sounds and letters used in formal Drac writings.

The wood eventually ran out. Jerry was very heavy and very, very sick as Zammis prepared to make its appearance, and it was all the Drac could do to waddle outside with my help to relieve itself. Hence, wood gathering, which involved taking our remaining stick and beating the ice off the dead standing trees, fell to me, as did cooking.

On a particularly blustery day, I noticed that the ice on the trees was thinner. Somewhere we had turned winter's corner and were heading for spring. I spent my ice-pounding time feeling great at the thought of spring, and I knew Jerry would pick up some at the news. The winter was really getting the Drac down. I was working the woods above the cave, taking armloads of gathered wood and dropping them down below, when I heard a scream. I froze, then looked around. I could see nothing but the sea and the ice around me. Then, the scream again. "Davidge!" It was Jerry. I dropped the load I was carrying and ran to the cleft in the cliff's face that served as a path to the upper woods. Jerry screamed again; and I slipped, then rolled until I came to the shelf level with the cave's mouth. I rushed through the entrance, down the passageway until I came to the chamber. Jerry writhed on its bed, digging its fingers into the sand.

I dropped on my knees next to the Drac. "I'm here, Jerry. What is it? What's wrong?"

"Davidge!" The Drac rolled its eyes, seeing nothing; its mouth worked silently, then exploded with another scream.

"Jerry, it's me!" I shook the Drac's shoulder. "It's me, Jerry. Davidge!"

Jerry turned its head toward me, grimaced, then clasped the fingers of one hand around my left wrist with the strength of pain. "Davidge! Zammis . . . something's gone wrong!"

"What? What can I do?"

Jerry screamed again, then its head fell back to the bed in a half-faint. The Drac fought back to consciousness and pulled my head down to its lips. "Davidge, you must swear."

"What, Jerry? Swear what?"

"Zammis . . . on Draco. To stand before the line's archives. Do this."

"What do you mean? You talk like you're dying."

"I am, Davidge. Zammis two-hundredth generation . . . very important. Present my child, Davidge. Swear!"

I wiped the sweat from my face with my free hand. "You're not going to die, Jerry. Hang on!"

"Enough! Face truth, Davidge! I die! You must teach the line of Jeriba to Zammis . . . and the book, the *Talman, gavey*?"

"Stop it!" Panic stood over me almost as a physical presence. "Stop talking like that! You aren't going to die, Jerry. Come on; fight, you *kizlode* sonofabitch . . ."

Jerry screamed. Its breathing was weak and the Drac drifted in and out of consciousness. "Davidge."

"What?" I realized I was sobbing like a kid.

"Davidge, you must help Zammis come out."

"What . . . how? What in the Hell are you talking about?"

Jerry turned its face to the wall of the cave. "Lift my jacket."

"What?"

"Lift my jacket, Davidge. Now!"

I pulled up the snakeskin jacket, exposing Jerry's swollen belly. The fold down the center was bright red and seeping a clear liquid. "What . . . what should I do?"

Jerry breathed rapidly, then held its breath. "Tear it open! You must tear it open, Davidge!"

"No!"

"Do it! Do it, or Zammis dies!"

"What do I care about your goddamn child, Jerry? What do I have to do to save you?"

"Tear it open . . ." whispered the Drac. "Take care of my child, *Irkmaan*. Present Zammis before the Jeriba archives. Swear this to me."

"Oh, Jerry . . ."

"Swear this!"

I nodded, hot fat tears dribbling down my cheeks. "I swear it. . . ." Jerry relaxed its grip on my wrist and closed its eyes. I knelt next to the Drac, stunned. "No. No, no, no, no."

Tear it open! You must tear it open, Davidge!

I reached up a hand and gingerly touched the fold on Jerry's belly. I could feel life struggling beneath it, trying to escape the airless confines of the Drac's womb. I hated it; I hated the damned thing as I never hated anything before. Its struggles grew weaker, then stopped.

Present Zammis before the Jeriba archives. Swear this to me. . . .

I swear it. . . .

I lifted my other hand and inserted my thumbs into the fold and tugged gently. I increased the amount of force, then tore at Jerry's belly like a madman. The fold burst open, soaking the front of my jacket with the clear fluid. Holding the fold open, I could see the still form of Zammis huddled in a well of the fluid, motionless.

I vomited. When I had nothing more to throw up, I reached into the fluid and put my hands under the Drac infant. I lifted it, wiped my mouth on my upper left sleeve, and closed my mouth over Zammis's and pulled the child's mouth open with my right hand. Three times, four times, I inflated the child's lungs, then it coughed. Then it cried. I tied off the two umbilicals with berrybush fiber, then cut them. Jeriba Zammis was freed of the dead flesh of its parent.

I held the rock over my head, then brought it down with all of my force upon the ice. Shards splashed away from the point of impact, exposing the dark green beneath. Again, I lifted the rock and brought it down, knocking loose another rock. I picked it up, stood and carried it to the half-covered corpse of the Drac. "The Drac," I whispered. *Good. Just call it "the Drac." Toadface. Dragger.*

The enemy. Call it anything to insulate those feelings against the pain.

I looked at the pile of rocks I had gathered, decided it was sufficient to finish the job, then knelt next to the grave. As I placed the rocks on the pile, unmindful of the gale-blown sleet freezing on my

snakeskins, I fought back the tears. I smacked my
hands together to help restore the circulation.
Spring was coming, but it was still dangerous to
stay outside too long. And I had been a long time
building the Drac's grave. I picked up another rock
and placed it into position. As the rock's weight
leaned against the snakeskin mattress cover, I
realized that the Drac was already frozen. I quickly
placed the remainder of the rocks, then stood.

The wind rocked me and I almost lost my footing
on the ice next to the grave. I looked toward the
boiling sea, pulled my snakeskins around myself
more tightly, then looked down at the pile of rocks.
*There should be words. You don't just cover up the
dead, then go to dinner. There should be words.* But
what words? I was no religionist, and neither was
the Drac. Its formal philosophy on the matter of
death was the same as my informal rejection of
Islamic delights, pagan Valhallas, and Judeo-
Christian pies in the sky. Death is death; *finis*; the
end; the worms crawl in, the worms crawl out . . .
Still, there should be words.

I reached beneath my snakeskins and clasped
my gloved hand around the golden cube of the
Talman. I felt the sharp corners of the cube
through my glove, closed my eyes, and ran through
the words of the great Drac philosophers. But there
was nothing they had written for this moment.

The *Talman* was a book on life. *Talman* means
"life," and this occupies Drac philosophy. They
spare nothing for death. Death is a fact; the end of
life. The *Talman* had no words for me to say. The
wind knifed through me, causing me to shiver.
Already my fingers were numb and pains were
beginning in my feet. Still, there should be words.
But the only words I could think of would open the

gate, flooding my being with pain—with the real-ization that the Drac was gone. *Still . . . still, there should be words.*

"Jerry, I . . ." I had no words. I turned from the grave, my tears mixing with the sleet.

With the warmth and silence of the cave around me, I sat on my mattress, my back against the wall of the cave. I tried to lose myself in the shadows and flickers of light cast on the opposite wall by the fire. Images would half-form, then dance away before I could move my mind to see something in them. As a child I used to watch clouds, and in them see faces, castles, animals, dragons, and giants. It was a world of escape—fantasy; some-thing to inject wonder and adventure into the mundane, regulated life of a middle-class boy leading a middle-class life. All I could see on the wall of the cave was a representation of Hell: flames licking at twisted, grotesque representa-tions of condemned souls. I laughed at the thought. We think of Hell as fire, supervised by a cackling sadist in a red union suit. Fyrine IV taught me this much: Hell is loneliness, hunger, and endless cold.

I heard a whimper, and I looked into the shad-ows toward the small mattress at the back of the cave. Jerry had made the snakeskin sack filled with seed pod down for Zammis. It whimpered again, and I leaned forward, wondering if there was something it needed. A pang of fear tickled my guts. What does a Drac infant eat? Dracs aren't mammals. All they ever taught us in training was how to recognize Dracs—that, and how to kill them. Then real fear began working on me. "What in the hell am I going to use for diapers?"

It whimpered again. I pushed myself to my feet, walked the sandy floor to the infant's side, then knelt beside it. Out of the bundle that was Jerry's old flight suit, two chubby three-fingered arms waved. I picked up the bundle, carried it next to the fire, and sat on a rock. Balancing the bundle on my lap, I carefully unwrapped it. I could see the yellow glitter of Zammis's eyes beneath yellow, sleep-heavy lids. From the almost noseless face and solid teeth to its deep yellow color, Zammis was every bit a miniature of Jerry, except for the fat. Zammis fairly wallowed in rolls of fat. I looked, and was grateful to find that there was no mess.

I looked into Zammis's face. "You want something to eat?"

"Guh."

Its jaws were ready for business, and I assumed that Dracs must chew solid food from day one. I reached over the fire and picked up a twist of dried snake, then touched it against the infant's lips. Zammis turned its head. "C'mon, eat. You're not going to find anything better around here."

I pushed the snake against its lips again, and Zammis pulled back a chubby arm and pushed it away. I shrugged. "Well, whenever you get hungry enough, it's there."

"Guh meh!" Its head rocked back and forth on my lap, a tiny, three-fingered hand closed around my finger, and it whimpered again.

"You don't want to eat, you don't need to be cleaned up, so what do you want? *Kos va nu?*"

Zammis's face wrinkled, and its hand pulled at my finger. Its other hand waved in the direction of my chest. I picked Zammis up to arrange the flight suit, and the tiny hands reached out, grasped the front of my snakeskins, and held on as the chubby arms pulled the child next to my chest. I held it close, it placed its cheek against my chest, and promptly fell asleep. "Well . . . I'll be damned."

Until the Drac was gone, I never realized how closely I had stood near the edge of madness. My loneliness was a cancer—a growth that I fed with hate: hate for the planet with its endless cold, endless winds, and endless isolation; hate for the helpless yellow child with its clawing need for care, food, and an affection that I couldn't give; and hate for myself. I found myself doing things that frightened and disgusted me. To break my solid wall of being alone, I would talk, shout, and sing to myself—uttering curses, nonsense, or meaningless croaks.

Its eyes were open, and it waved a chubby arm and cooed. I picked up a large rock, staggered over to the child's side, and held the weight over the tiny body. "I could drop this thing, kid. Where would you be then?" I felt laughter coming from my lips. I threw the rock aside. "Why should I mess up the cave? Outside. Put you outside for a minute, and you die! You hear me? Die!"

The child worked its three-fingered hands at the empty air, shut its eyes, and cried. "Why don't you eat? Why don't you crap? Why don't you do anything right, but cry?" The child cried more loudly. "Bah! I ought to pick up that rock and finish it! That's what I ought . . ." A wave of revulsion stopped my words, and I went to my mattress, picked up my cap, gloves, and muff, then headed outside.

Before I came to the rocked-in entrance to the cave, I felt the bite of the wind. Outside I stopped and looked at the sea and sky—a roiling panorama in glorious black and white, grey and grey. A gust of wind slapped against me, rocking me back toward the entrance. I regained my balance, walked to the edge of the cliff, and shook my fist at the sea. "Go ahead! Go ahead and blow, you *kizlode* sonofabitch! You haven't killed me yet!"

I squeezed the wind-burned lids of my eyes shut, then opened them and looked down. A forty-meter drop to the next ledge, but if I took a running jump, I could clear it. Then it would be a hundred and fifty meters to the rocks below. *Jump.* I backed away from the cliff's edge. "Jump! Sure, jump!" I shook my head at the sea. "I'm not going to do your job for you! You want me dead, you're going to have to do it yourself!"

I looked back and up, above the entrance to the cave. The sky was darkening and in a few hours night would shroud the landscape. I turned toward the cleft in the rock that led to the scrub forest above the cave.

I squatted next to the Drac's grave and studied the rocks I had placed there, already fused together with a layer of ice. "Jerry. What am I going to do?"

The Drac would sit by the fire, both of us sewing. And we talked.

"You know, Jerry, all this," I held up the Talman, "I've heard it all before. I expected something different."

The Drac lowered its sewing to its lap and studied

me for an instant. Then it shook its head and resumed its sewing. "You are not a terribly profound creature, Davidge."

"What's that supposed to mean?"

Jerry held out a three-fingered hand. "A universe, Davidge—there is a universe out there, a universe of life, objects, and events. There are differences, but it is all the same universe, and we all must obey the same universal laws. Did you ever think of that?"

"No."

"That is what I mean, Davidge. Not terribly profound."

I snorted. "I told you, I'd heard this stuff before. So I imagine that shows humans to be just as profound as Dracs."

Jerry laughed. "You always insist on making something racial out of my observations. What I said applied to you, not to the race of humans. . . ."

I spat on the frozen ground. "You Dracs think you're so damned smart." The wind picked up, and I could taste the sea salt in it. One of the big blows was coming. The sky was changing to that curious darkness that tricked me into thinking it was midnight blue, rather than black. A trickle of ice found its way under my collar.

"What's wrong with me just being me? Everybody in the universe doesn't have to be a damned philosopher, toadface!" There were millions—billions—like me. More maybe. "What difference does it make to anything whether I ponder existence or not? It's here; that's all I have to know."

"Davidge, you don't even know your family line beyond your parents, and now you say you refuse to know that of your universe that you can know. How will you know your place in this existence, Davidge? Where are you? Who are you?"

I shook my head and stared at the grave, then I turned and faced the sea. In another hour, or less, it would be too dark to see the whitecaps. "I'm me, that's who." But was that "me" who held the rock over Zammis, threatening a helpless infant with death? I felt my guts curdle as the loneliness I thought I felt grew claws and fangs and began gnawing and slashing at the remains of my sanity. I turned back to the grave, closed my eyes, then opened them. "I'm a fighter pilot, Jerry. Isn't that something?"

"That is what you do, Davidge; that is neither who nor what you are."

I knelt next to the grave and clawed at the ice-sheathed rocks with my hands. "You don't talk to me now, Drac! *You're dead!*" I stopped, realizing that the words I had heard were from the *Talman*, processed into my own context. I slumped against the rocks, felt the wind, then pushed myself to my feet. "Jerry, Zammis won't eat. It's been three days. What do I do? Why didn't you tell me anything about Drac brats before you . . ." I held my hands to my face. "Steady, boy. Keep it up, and they'll stick you in a home." The wind pressed against my back, I lowered my hands, then walked from the grave.

I sat in the cave, staring at the fire. I couldn't hear the wind through the rock, and the wood was dry, making the fire hot and quiet. I tapped my fingers against my knee, then began humming. Noise, any kind, helped to drive off the oppressive loneliness. "Sonofabitch." I laughed and nodded. "Yea, verily, and *kizlode va nu, dutschaat.*" I chuckled, trying to think of all the curses and obscenities in Drac that I had learned from Jerry. There were quite a few. My toe tapped against the sand and my humming started up again. I stopped, frowned, then remembered the song.

> "Highty tighty Christ almighty,
> Who the Hell are we?
> Zim zam, Gawd Damn,
> We're in Squadron B."

I leaned back against the wall of the cave, trying to remember another verse. *A pilot's got a rotten life/ no crumpets with our tea/ we have to service the general's wife/ and pick fleas from her knee.* "Damn!" I slapped my knee, trying to see the faces of the other pilots in the squadron lounge. I could almost feel the whiskey fumes tickling the inside of my nose. Vadik, Wooster, Arnold—the one with the broken nose—Demerest, Kadiz. I hummed again, swinging an imaginary mug of issue grog by its imaginary handle.

> "And, if he doesn't like it,
> I'll tell you what we'll do:
> We'll fill his ass with broken glass,
> and seal it up with glue."

The cave echoed with the song. I stood, threw up my arms and screamed. "Yaaaaahoooooo!"

Zammis began crying. I bit my lip and walked over to the bundle on the mattress. "Well? You ready to eat?"

"Unh, unh, weh." The infant rocked its head back and forth. I went to the fire, picked up a twist of snake, then returned. I knelt next to Zammis

and held the snake to its lips. Again, the child
pushed it away. "Come on, you. You have to eat." I
tried again with the same results. I took the wraps
off the child and looked at its body. I could tell it
was losing weight, although Zammis didn't appear
to be getting weak. I shrugged, wrapped it up
again, stood, and began walking back to my mattress.

"Guh, weh."

I turned. "What?"

"Ah, guh, guh."

I went back, stooped over and picked the child
up. Its eyes were open and it looked into my face,
then smiled.

"What're you laughing at, ugly? You should get a
load of your own face."

Zammis barked out a short laugh, then gurgled.
I went to my mattress, sat down, and arranged
Zammis in my lap. "Gumma, buh, buh." Its hand
grabbed a loose flap of snakeskin on my shirt and
pulled on it.

"Gumma, buh, buh to you, too. So, what do we
do now? How about I start teaching you the line of
Jeriban? You're going to have to learn it sometime,
and it might as well be now." The Jeriban line. My
recitations of the line were the only things Jerry
ever complimented me about. I looked into
Zammis's eyes. "When I bring you to stand before
the Jeriba archives, you will say this: 'Before you
here I stand, Zammis of the line of Jeriba, born of
Shigan, the fighter pilot.'" I smiled, thinking of the
upraised yellow brows if Zammis continued, *"and,
by damn, Shigan was a helluva good pilot, too. Why,
I was once told he took a smart round in his tail
feathers, then pulled around and rammed the*
kizlode *sonofabitch, known to one and all as Willis
E. Davidge . . ."* I shook my head. "You're not going

to get your wings by doing the line in English, Zammis." I began again:

"Naatha nu enta va, Zammis zea does Jeriba, estay va Shigan, asaam naa denvadar. . . ."

For eight of those long days and nights, I feared the child would die. I tried everything—roots, dried berries, dried plumfruit, snakemeat dried, boiled, chewed, and ground. Zammis refused it all. I checked frequently, but each time I looked through the child's wraps, they were as clean as when I had put them on. Zammis lost weight, but seemed to grow stronger. By the ninth day it was crawling the floor of the cave. Even with the fire, the cave wasn't really warm. I feared that the kid would get sick crawling around naked, and I dressed it in the tiny snakeskin suit and cap Jerry had made for it. After dressing it, I stood Zammis up and looked at it. The kid had already developed a smile full of mischief that, combined with the twinkle in its yellow eyes and its suit and cap, make it look like an elf. I was holding Zammis up in a standing position. The kid seemed pretty steady on its legs, and I let go. Zammis smiled, waved its thinning arms about, then laughed and took a faltering step toward me. I caught it as it fell, and the little Drac squealed.

In two more days Zammis was walking and getting into everything that could be gotten into. I spent many an anxious moment searching the chambers at the back of the cave for the kid after coming in from outside. Finally, when I caught it at the mouth of the cave heading full steam for the outside, I had had enough. I made a harness out of snakeskin, attached it to a snake-leather leash, and tied the other end to a projection of rock above my head. Zammis still got into everything, but at least I could find it.

Four days after it learned to walk, it wanted to eat. Drac babies are probably the most convenient and considerate infants in the universe. They live off their fat for about three or four Earth weeks, and don't make a mess the entire time. After they learn to walk, and can therefore make it to a mutually agreed upon spot, then they want food and begin discharging wastes. I showed the kid once how to use the litter box I had made, and never had to again. After five or six lessons, Zammis was handling its own drawers. Watching the little Drac learn and grow, I began to understand those pilots in my squadron who used to bore each other—and everyone else—with countless pictures of ugly children, accompanied by thirty-minute narratives for each snapshot. Before the ice melted, Zammis was talking. I taught it to call me "Uncle."

For lack of a better term, I called the ice-melting season "spring." It would be a long time before the scrub forest showed any green or the snakes ventured forth from their icy holes. The sky maintained its eternal cover of dark, angry clouds, and still the sleet would come and coat everything with a hard, slippery glaze. But the next day the glaze would melt, and the warmer air would push another millimeter into the soil.

I realized that this was the time to be gathering wood. Before the winter hit, Jerry and I working together hadn't gathered enough wood. The short summer would have to be spent putting up food for the next winter. I was hoping to build a tighter door over the mouth of the cave, and I swore that I would figure out some kind of indoor plumbing. Dropping your drawers outside in the middle of winter was dangerous. My mind was full of these things as I stretched out on my mattress watching the smoke curl through a crack in the roof of the cave. Zammis was off in the back of the cave playing with some rocks that it had found, and I must have fallen asleep. I awoke with the kid shaking my arm.

"Uncle?"

"Huh? Zammis?"

"Uncle. Look."

I rolled over on my left side and faced the Drac. Zammis was holding up its right hand, fingers spread out. "What is it, Zammis?"

"Look." It pointed at each of its three fingers in turn. "One, two, three."

"So?"

"Look." Zammis grabbed my right hand and spread out the fingers. "One, two, three, *four, five!*"

I nodded. "So you can count to five."

The Drac frowned and made an impatient gesture with its tiny fists. "Look." It took my outstretched hand and placed its own on top of it. With its other hand, Zammis pointed first at one of its own fingers, then at one of mine. "One, one." The child's yellow eyes studied me to see if I understood.

"Yes."

The child pointed again. "Two, two." It looked at me, then looked back at my hand and pointed. "Three, three." Then he grabbed my two remaining fingers. *"Four, five?"* It dropped my hand, then pointed to the side of its own hand. "Four, five?"

I shook my head. Zammis, at less than four Earth months old, had detected part of the difference between Dracs and humans. A human child would be—what—five, six, or seven years old before asking questions like that. I sighed. "Zammis."

"Yes, Uncle?"

"Zammis, you are a Drac. Dracs only have three fingers on a hand." I held up my right hand and wiggled the fingers. "I'm a human. I have five."

I swear that tears welled in the child's eyes. Zammis held out its hands, looked at them, then shook its head. "Grow four, five?"

I sat up and faced the kid. Zammis was wondering where its other four fingers had gone. "Look, Zammis. You and I are different . . . different kinds of beings, understand?"

Zammis shook his head. "Grow four, five?"

"You won't. You're a Drac." I pointed at my chest. "I'm a human." This was getting me nowhere. "Your parent, where you came from, was a Drac. Do you understand?"

Zammis frowned. "Drac. What Drac?"

The urge to resort to the timeless standby of "you'll understand when you get older" pounded at the back of my mind. I shook my head. "Dracs have three fingers on each hand. Your parent had three fingers on each hand." I rubbed my beard. "My parent was a human and had five fingers on each hand. That's why I have five fingers on each hand."

Zammis knelt on the sand and studied its fingers. It looked up at me, back to its hands, then back to me. "What parent?"

I studied the kid. It must be having an identity crisis of some kind. I was the only person it had ever seen, and I had five fingers per hand. "A parent is . . . the thing . . ." I scratched my beard again. "Look . . . we all come from someplace. I had a mother and father—two different kinds of humans—that gave me life; that made me, understand?"

Zammis gave me a look that could be interpreted as "Mac, you are full of it." I shrugged. "I don't know if I can explain it."

Zammis pointed at its own chest. "My mother? My father?"

I held out my hands, dropped them into my lap, pursed my lips, scratched my beard, and generally stalled for time. Zammis held an unblinking gaze on me the entire time. "Look, Zammis. You don't have a mother and a father. I'm a human, so I have them; you're a Drac. You have a parent—just one, see?"

Zammis shook its head. It looked at me, then pointed at its own chest. "Drac."

"Right."

Zammis pointed at my chest. "Human."

"Right again."

Zammis removed its hand and dropped it in its lap. "Where Drac come from?"

Sweet Jesus! Trying to explain hermaphroditic reproduction to a kid who shouldn't even be crawling yet! "Zammis . . ." I held up my hands, then dropped them into my lap. "Look. You see how much bigger I am than you?"

"Yes, Uncle."

"Good." I ran my fingers through my hair, fighting for time and inspiration. "Your parent was big, like me. Its name was . . . Jeriba Shigan." Funny how just saying the name was painful. "Jeriba Shigan was like you. It only had three fingers on each hand. It grew you in its tummy." I poked Zammis's middle. "Understand?"

Zammis giggled and held its hands over its stomach. "Uncle, how Dracs grow there?"

I lifted my legs onto the mattress and stretched out. Where do little Dracs come from? I looked over to Zammis and saw the child hanging upon my every word. I grimaced and told the truth. "Damned if I know, Zammis. Damned if I know." Thirty seconds later, Zammis was back playing with its rocks.

Summer, and I taught Zammis how to capture and skin the long grey snakes, and then how to smoke the meat. The child would squat on the shallow bank above a mudpool, its yellow eyes fixed on the snake holes in the bank, waiting for one of the occupants to poke out its head. The wind would blow, but Zammis wouldn't move. Then a flat, triangular head set with tiny blue eyes would appear. The snake would check the pool, turn and check the bank, then check the sky. It would advance out of the hole a bit, then check it all again. Often the snakes would look directly at Zammis, but the Drac could have been carved from rock. Zammis wouldn't move until the snake was too far out of the hole to pull itself back in tail first. Then Zammis would strike, grabbing the snake with both hands just behind the head. The snakes had no fangs and weren't poisonous, but they were lively enough to toss Zammis into the mudpool on occasion.

The skins were spread and wrapped around tree trunks and pegged in place to dry. The tree trunks were kept in an open place near the entrance to the cave, but under an overhang that faced away from the ocean. About two thirds of the skins put up in this manner cured; the remaining third would rot.

Beyond the skin room was the smokehouse: a rock-walled chamber that we would hang with rows of snakemeat. A greenwood fire would be set in a pit in the chamber's floor; then we would fill in the small opening with rocks and dirt.

"Uncle, why doesn't the meat rot after it's smoked?"

I thought upon it. "I'm not sure; I just know it doesn't."

"Why do you know?"

I shrugged. "I just do. I read about it, probably."

"What's read?"

"Reading. Like when I sit down and read the *Talman*."

"Does the *Talman* say why the meat doesn't rot?"

"No. I meant that I probably read it in another book."

"Do we have more books?"

I shook my head. "I meant before I came to this planet."

"Why did you come to this planet?"

"I told you. Your parent and I were stranded here during the battle."

"Why do the humans and Dracs fight?"

"It's very complicated." I waved my hands about for a bit. The human line was that the Dracs were aggressors invading our space. The Drac line was that the humans were aggressors invading their space. The truth? "Zammis, it has to do with the colonization of new planets. Both races are expanding and both races have a tradition of exploring and colonizing new planets. I guess we just expanded into each other. Understand?"

Zammis nodded, then became mercifully silent as it fell into deep thought. The main thing I learned from the Drac child was all of the ques-

tions I didn't have answers to. I was feeling very smug, however, at having gotten Zammis to understand about the war, thereby avoiding my ignorance on the subject of preserving meat. "Uncle?"
   "Yes, Zammis?"
   "What's a planet?"

   As the cold, wet summer came to an end, we had the cave jammed with firewood and preserved food. With that out of the way, I concentrated my efforts on making some kind of indoor plumbing out of the natural pools in the chambers deep within the cave. The bathtub was no problem. By dropping heated rocks into one of the pools, the water could be brought up to a bearable—even comfortable—temperature. After bathing, the hollow stems of a bamboolike plant could be used to siphon out the dirty water. The tub could then be refilled from the pool above. The problem was where to siphon the water. Several of the chambers had holes in their floors. The first three holes we tried drained into our main chamber, wetting the low edge near the entrance. The previous winter, Jerry and I had considered using one of those holes for a toilet that we would flush with water from the pools. Since we didn't know where the goodies would come out, we decided against it.
   The fourth hole Zammis and I tried drained out below the entrance to the cave in the face of the cliff. Not ideal, but better than answering the call of nature in the middle of a combination ice storm and blizzard. We rigged up the hole as a drain for both the tub and toilet. As Zammis and I prepared to enjoy our first hot bath, I removed my snakeskins, tested the water with my toe, then stepped

in. "Great!" I turned to Zammis, the child still half dressed. "Come on in, Zammis. The water's fine." Zammis was staring at me, its mouth hanging open. "What's the matter?"

The child stared wide-eyed, then pointed at me with a three-fingered hand. "Uncle . . . what's that?"

I looked down. "Oh." I shook my head, then looked up at the child. "Zammis, I explained all that, remember? I'm a human."

"But what's it *for*?"

I sat down in the warm water, removing the object of discussion from sight. "It's for the elimination of liquid wastes . . . among other things. Now, hop in and get washed."

Zammis shucked its snakeskins, looked down at its own smooth-surfaced, combined system, then climbed into the tube. The child settled into the water up to its neck, its yellow eyes studying me. "Uncle?"

"Yes?"

"What *other things*?"

Well, I told Zammis. For the first time, the Drac appeared to be trying to decide whether my response was truthful or not, rather than its usual acceptance of my every assertion. In fact, I was convinced that Zammis thought I was lying— probably because I was.

Winter began with a sprinkle of snowflakes carried on a gentle breeze. I took Zammis above the cave to the scrub forest. I held the child's hand as we stood before the pile of rocks that served as Jerry's grave. Zammis pulled its snakeskins against the wind, bowed its head, then turned and looked up into my face. "Uncle, this is the grave of my parent?"

I nodded. "Yes."

Zammis turned back to the grave, then shook its head. "Uncle, how should I feel?"

"I don't understand, Zammis."

The child nodded at the grave. "I can see that you are sad being here. I think you want me to feel the same. Do you?"

I frowned, then shook my head. "No. I don't want you to be sad. I just wanted you to know where it is."

"May I go now?"

"Sure. Are you certain you know the way back to the cave?"

"Yes. I just want to make sure my soap doesn't burn again."

I watched as the child turned and scurried off into the naked trees, then I turned back to the grave. "Well, Jerry, what do you think of your kid? Zammis was using wood ashes to clean the grease off the shells, then it put a shell back on the fire and put water in it to boil off the burnt-on food. Fat and ashes. The next thing, Jerry, we were making soap. Zammis's first batch almost took the hide off us, but the kid's getting better . . ."

I looked up at the clouds, then brought my glance down to the sea. In the distance, low, dark clouds were building up. "See that? You know what that means, don't you? Ice storm number one." The wind picked up and I squatted next to the grave to replace a rock that had rolled from the pile. "Zammis is a good kid, Jerry. I wanted to hate it . . . after you died. I wanted to hate it." I replaced the rock, then looked back toward the sea.

"I don't know how we're going to make it off

planet, Jerry—" I caught a flash of movement out of the corner of my vision. I turned to the right and looked over the tops of the trees. Against the grey sky, a black speck streaked away. I followed it with my eyes until it went above the clouds.

I listened, hoping to hear an exhaust roar, but my heart was pounding so hard, all I could hear was the wind. Was it a ship? I stood, took a few steps in the direction the speck was going, then stopped. Turning my head, I saw that the rocks on Jerry's grave were already capped with thin layers of fine snow. I shrugged and headed for the cave. "Probably just a bird."

Zammis sat on its mattress, stabbing several pieces of snakeskin with a bone needle. I stretched out on my own mattress and watched the smoke curl up toward the crack in the ceiling. Was it a bird? Or was it a ship? Damn, but it worked on me. Escape from the planet had been out of my thoughts, had been buried, hidden for all that summer. But again, it twisted at me. To walk where a sun shined, to wear cloth again, experience central heating, eat food prepared by a chef, to be among . . . people again.

I rolled over on my right side and stared at the wall next to my mattress. People. Human people. I closed my eyes and swallowed. Girl human people. Female persons. Images drifted before my eyes— faces, bodies, laughing couples, the dance after flight training . . . what was her name? Dolora? Dora?

I shook my head, rolled over and sat up, facing the fire. Why did I have to see whatever it was? All those things I had been able to bury—to forget—boiling over.

"Uncle?"

I looked up at Zammis. Yellow skin, yellow eyes, noseless toad face. I shook my head. "What?"

"Is something wrong?"

Is something wrong, hah. "No. I just thought I saw something today. It probably wasn't anything." I reached to the fire and took a piece of dried snake from the griddle. I blew on it, then gnawed on the stringy strip.

"What did it look like?"

"I don't know. The way it moved, I thought it might be a ship. It went away so fast, I couldn't be sure. Might have been a bird."

"Bird?"

I studied Zammis. It'd never seen a bird; neither had I on Fyrine IV. "An animal that flies."

Zammis nodded. "Uncle, when we were gathering wood up in the scrub forest, I saw something fly."

"What? Why didn't you tell me?"

"I meant to, but I forgot."

"Forgot!" I frowned. "In which direction was it going?"

Zammis pointed to the back of the cave. "That way. Away from the sea." Zammis put down its sewing. "Can we go see where it went?"

I shook my head. "The winter is just beginning. You don't know what it's like. We'd die in only a few days."

Zammis went back to poking holes in the snakeskin. To make the trek in the winter would kill us. But spring would be something else. We could survive with double layered snakeskins stuffed with seed pod down, and a tent. We had to have a tent. Zammis and I could spend the winter making it, and packs. Boots. We'd need sturdy walking boots. Have to think on that . . .

It's strange how a spark of hope can ignite, and spread, until all desperation is consumed. Was it a ship? I didn't know. If it was, was it taking off, or landing? I didn't know. If it was taking off, we'd be heading in the wrong direction. But the opposite direction meant crossing the sea. Whatever. Come spring we would head beyond the scrub forest and see what was there.

The winter seemed to pass quickly, with Zammis occupied with the tent and my time devoted to rediscovering the art of boot making. I made tracings of both of our feet on snakeskin, and, after some experimentation, I found that boiling the snake leather with plumfruit made it soft and gummy. By taking several of the gummy layers, weighting them, then setting them aside to dry, the result was a tough, flexible sole. By the time I finished Zammis's boots, the Drac needed a new pair.

"They're too small, Uncle."

"Waddaya mean, too small?"

Zammis pointed down. "They hurt. My toes are all crippled up."

I squatted down and felt the tops over the child's toes. "I don't understand. It's only been twenty, twenty-five days since I made the tracings. You sure you didn't move when I made them?"

Zammis shook its head. "I didn't move."

I frowned, then stood. "Stand up, Zammis." The Drac stood and I moved next to it. The top of

Zammis's head came to the middle of my chest. Another sixty centimeters and it'd be as tall as Jerry. "Take them off, Zammis. I'll make a bigger pair. Try not to grow so fast."

Zammis pitched the tent inside the cave, put glowing coals inside, then rubbed fat into the leather for waterproofing. It had grown taller, and I had held off making the Drac's boots until I could be sure of the size it would need. I tried to do a projection by measuring Zammis's feet every ten days, then extending the curve into spring. According to my figures, the kid would have feet resembling a pair of attack transports by the time the snow melted. By spring, Zammis would be full grown. Jerry's old flight boots had fallen apart before Zammis had been born, but I had saved the pieces. I used the soles to make my tracings and hoped for the best.

I was busy with the new boots and Zammis was keeping an eye on the tent treatment. The Drac looked back at me.

"Uncle?"

"What?"

"Existence is the first given?"

I shrugged. "That's what Shizumaat says; I'll buy it."

"But, Uncle, how do we *know* that existence is real?"

I lowered my work, looked at Zammis, shook my head, then resumed stitching the boots. "Take my word for it."

The Drac grimaced. "But, Uncle, that is not knowledge; that is faith."

I sighed, thinking back to my sophomore year at the University of Nations—a bunch of adolescents lounging around a cheap flat experimenting with booze, powders, and philosophy. At a little more than one Earth year old, Zammis was developing into an intellectual bore. "So, what's wrong with faith?"

Zammis snickered. "Come now, Uncle. *Faith*?"

"It helps some of us along this drizzle-soaked coil."

"Coil?"

I scratched my head. "This mortal coil; life. Shakespeare, I think."

Zammis frowned. "It is not in the *Talman*."

"He, not it. Shakespeare was a human."

Zammis stood, walked to the fire and sat across from me. "Was he a philosopher, like Mistan or Shizumaat?"

"No. He wrote plays—like stories, acted out."

Zammis rubbed its chin. "Do you remember any of Shakespeare?"

I held up a finger. " 'To be, or not to be; that is the question.' "

The Drac's mouth dropped open; then it nodded its head. "Yes. Yes! To be or not to be; that *is* the question!" Zammis held out its hands. "How do we *know* the wind blows outside the cave when we are not there to see it? Does the sea still boil if we are not there to feel it?"

I nodded. "Yes."

"But, Uncle, how do we *know*?"

I squinted at the Drac. "Zammis, I have a question for you. Is the following statement true or false: What I am saying right now is false."

Zammis blinked. "If it is false, then the statement is true. But . . . if it's true . . . the statement is false, but . . ." Zammis blinked again, then turned and went back to rubbing fat into the tent. "I'll think upon it, Uncle."

"You do that, Zammis."

The Drac thought upon it for about ten minutes, then turned back. "The statement is false."

I smiled. "But that's what the statement said, hence it is true, but . . ." I let the puzzle trail off. Oh, smugness, thou temptest even saints.

"No, Uncle. The statement is meaningless in its present context." I shrugged. "You see, Uncle, the statement assumes the existence of truth values that can comment upon themselves devoid of any other reference. I think Lurrvena's logic in the *Talman* is clear on this, and if meaninglessness is equated with falsehood . . ."

I sighed. "Yeah, well—"

"You see, Uncle, you must first establish a context in which your statement has meaning."

I leaned forward, frowned, and scratched my beard. "I see. You mean I was putting Descartes before the horse?"

Zammis looked at me strangely, and even more so when I collapsed on my mattress cackling like a fool.

"Uncle, why does the line of Jeriba have only five names? You say that human lines have many names."

I nodded. "The five names of the Jeriba line are things to which their bearers must add deeds. The deeds are important—not the names."

"Gothig is Shigan's parent as Shigan is my parent."

"Of course. You know that from your recitations."

Zammis frowned. "Then I *must* name my child Ty when I become a parent?"

"Yes. And Ty must name its child Haesni. Do you see something wrong with that?"

"I would like to name my child Davidge, after you."

I smiled and shook my head. "The Ty name has been served by great bankers, merchants, inventors, and—well, you know your recitation. The name Davidge hasn't been served by much. Think of what Ty would miss by not being Ty."

Zammis thought a while, then nodded. "Uncle, do you think Gothig is alive?"

"As far as I know."

"What is Gothig like?"

I thought back to Jerry talking about its parent, Gothig. "It taught music, and is very strong. Jerry . . . Shigan said that its parent could bend metal bars with its fingers. Gothig is also very dignified. I imagine that right now Gothig is also very sad. Gothig must think that the line of Jeriba has ended."

Zammis frowned and its yellow brow furrowed. "Uncle, we must make it to Draco. We must tell Gothig the line continues."

"We will."

The winter's ice began thinning, and boots, tent, and packs were ready. We were putting the finishing touches on our new insulated suits. As Jerry had given the *Talman* to me to learn, the golden cube now hung around Zammis's neck. The Drac would drop the tiny golden book from the cube and study it for hours at a time.

"Uncle?"

"What?"

"Why do Dracs speak and write in one language and the humans in another?"

I laughed. "Zammis, the humans speak and write in many languages. English is just one of them."

"How do the humans speak among themselves?"

I shrugged. "They don't always; when they do, they use interpreters—people who can speak both languages."

"You and I speak both English and Drac; does that make us interpreters?"

"I suppose we could be, if you could ever find a human and a Drac who want to talk to each other. Remember, there's a war going on."

"How will the war stop if they do not talk?"

"I suppose they will talk, eventually."

Zammis smiled. "I think I would like to be an interpreter and help end the war." The Drac put its sewing aside and stretched out on its new mattress. Zammis had outgrown even its old mattress, which it now used for a pillow. "Uncle, do you think that we will find anybody beyond the scrub forest?"

"I hope so."

"If we do, will you go with me to Draco?"

"I promised your parent that I would."

"I mean, after. After I make my recitation, what will you do?"

I stared at the fire. "I don't know." I shrugged. "The war might keep us from getting to Draco for a long time."

"After that, what?"

"I suppose I'll go back into the service."

Zammis propped itself up on an elbow. "Go back to being a fighter pilot?"

"Sure. That's about all I know how to do."

"And kill Dracs?"

I put my own sewing down and studied the Drac. Things had changed since Jerry and I had slugged it out—more things than I had realized. I shook my head. "No. I probably won't be a pilot—not a service one. Maybe I can land a job flying commercial ships." I shrugged. "Maybe the service won't give me any choice."

Zammis sat up, was still for a moment; then it stood, walked over to my mattress, and knelt before me on the sand. "Uncle, I don't want to leave you."

"Don't be silly. You'll have your own kind around you. Your grandparent, Gothig, Shigan's siblings, their children—you'll forget all about me."

"Will you forget about me?"

I looked into those yellow eyes, then reached out my hand and touched Zammis's cheek. "No, I won't forget about you. But, remember this, Zammis: you're a Drac and I'm a human, and that's how this part of the universe is divided."

Zammis took my hand from his cheek, spread the fingers and studied them. "Whatever happens, Uncle, I will never forget you."

The ice was gone, and the Drac and I stood in the wind-blown drizzle, packs on our backs, before the grave. Zammis was as tall as I was, which made it a little taller than Jerry. To my relief, the boots fit. Zammis hefted its pack up higher on its shoulders, then turned from the grave and looked out at the sea. I followed Zammis's glance and watched the rollers steam in and smash on the rocks. I looked at the Drac. "What are you thinking about?"

Zammis looked down, then turned toward me. "Uncle, I didn't think of it before, but . . . I will miss this place."

I laughed. "Nonsense! This place?" I slapped the Drac on the shoulder. "Why would you miss this place?"

Zammis looked back out to sea. "I have learned many things here. You have taught me many things here, Uncle. My life happened here."

"Only the beginning, Zammis. You have a life ahead of you." I nodded my head at the grave. "Say goodbye."

Zammis turned toward the grave, stood over it, then knelt to one side and began removing the rocks. After a few moments, it had exposed the hand of a skeleton with three fingers. Zammis nodded, then wept. "I am sorry, Uncle, but I had to do that. This has been nothing but a pile of rocks to me. Now it is more." Zammis replaced the rocks, then stood.

I cocked my head toward the scrub forest. "Go on ahead. I'll catch up in a minute."

"Yes, Uncle."

Zammis moved off toward the naked trees, and I looked down at the grave. "What do you think of Zammis, Jerry? It's bigger than you were. I guess snake agrees with the kid." I squatted next to the grave, picked up a small rock, and added it to the pile. "I guess this is it. We're either going to make it to Draco, or die trying." I stood and looked at the sea. "Yeah, I guess I learned a few things here. I'll miss it, in a way." I turned back to the grave and hefted my pack up. *"Ehdevva sahn, Jeriba Shigan.* So long, Jerry."

I turned and followed Zammis into the forest.

The days that followed were full of wonder for Zammis. For me the sky was still the same, dull grey, and the few variations of plant and animal life that we found were nothing remarkable. Once we got beyond the scrub forest, we climbed a gentle rise for a day, and then found ourselves on a wide, flat, endless plain. It was ankle deep in a purple weed that stained our boots the same color. The nights were still too cold for hiking, and we would hole up in the tent. Both the greased tent and suits worked well, keeping out the almost constant rain.

We had been out perhaps two of Fyrine IV's long weeks when we saw it. It screamed overhead, then disappeared over the horizon before either of us could say a word. I had no doubt that the craft I had seen was in landing attitude.

"Uncle! Did it see us?"

I shook my head. "No, I doubt it. But it was landing. Do you hear? It was landing somewhere ahead."

"Uncle?"

"Let's get moving! What is it?"

"Was it a Drac ship, or a human ship?"

I cooled in my tracks. I had never stopped to think about it. I waved my hand. "Come on. It doesn't matter. Either way, you go to Draco. You're a noncombatant, so the USE forces couldn't do anything, and if they're Dracs, you're home free."

We began walking. "But, Uncle, if it's a Drac ship, what will happen to you?"

I shrugged. "Prisoner of war. The Dracs say they abide by the interplanetary war accords, so I should be all right." *Fat chance*, said the back of my head to the front of my head. The big question was whether I preferred being a Drac POW or a permanent resident of Fyrine IV. I had figured that out long ago. "Come on, let's pick up the pace. We don't know how long it will take to get there, or how long it will be on the ground."

Pick 'em up; put 'em down. Except for a few breaks, we didn't stop—even when night came. Our exertion kept us warm. The horizon never seemed to grow nearer. The longer we slogged ahead the duller my mind grew. It must have been days, my mind gone numb as my feet, when I fell through the purple weed into a hole. Immediately, everything grew dark, and I felt a pain in my right leg. I felt the blackout coming, and I welcomed its warmth, its rest, its peace.

"Uncle? Uncle? Wake up! Please, wake up!"

I felt slapping against my face, although it felt somehow detached. Agony thundered into my brain, bringing me wide awake. Damned if I didn't break my leg. I looked up and saw the weedy edges of the hole. My rear end was seated in a trickle of water. Zammis squatted next to me.

"What happened?"

Zammis motioned upward. "This hole was only covered by a thin crust of dirt and plants. The water must have taken the ground away. Are you all right?"

"My leg. I think I broke it." I leaned my back

against the muddy wall. "Zammis, you're going to have to go on by yourself."

"I can't leave you, Uncle!"

"Look, if you find anyone, you can send them back for me."

"What if the water in here comes up?" Zammis felt along my leg until I winced. "I must carry you out of here. What must I do for the leg?"

The kid had a point. Drowning wasn't in my schedule. "We need something stiff. Bind the leg so it doesn't move."

Zammis pulled off its pack, and kneeling in the water and mud, went through its pack, then through the tent roll. Using the tent poles, it wrapped my leg with snakeskins torn from the tent. Then, using more snakeskins, Zammis made two loops, slipped one over each of my legs, then propped me up and slipped the loops over its shoulders. It lifted, and I blacked out.

I was on the ground, covered with the remains of the tent, and Zammis was shaking my arm. "Uncle? Uncle?"

"Yes?" I whispered.

"Uncle, I'm ready to go." It pointed to my side. "Your food is here, and when it rains, just pull the tent over your face. I'll mark the trail I make so I can find my way back."

I nodded. "Take care of yourself."

Zammis shook its head. "Uncle, I can carry you. We shouldn't separate."

I weakly shook my head. "Give me a break, kid. I couldn't make it. Find somebody and bring 'em back." I felt my stomach flip, and cold sweat drenched my snakeskins. "Go on; get going."

Zammis reached out, grabbed its pack, and

stood. The pack shouldered, Zammis turned and began running in the direction that the craft had been going. I watched until I couldn't see it. I faced up and looked at the clouds. "You almost got me that time, you *kizlode* sonofabitch, but you didn't figure on the Drac . . . you keep forgetting . . . there's two of us . . ." I drifted in and out of consciousness, felt rain on my face, then pulled up the tent and covered my head. In seconds, the blackout returned.

"Davidge? Lieutenant Davidge?"

I opened my eyes and saw something I hadn't seen for four Earth years: a human face. "Who are you?"

The face, young, long, and capped by short blond hair, smiled. "I'm Captain Steerman, the medical officer. How do you feel?"

I pondered the question and smiled. "Like I've been shot full of very high-grade junk."

"You have. You were in pretty bad shape by the time the survey team brought you in."

"Survey team?"

"I guess you don't know. The United States of Earth and the Dracon Chamber have established a joint commission to supervise the colonization of new planets. The war is over."

"Over?"

"Yes."

Something heavy lifted from my chest. "Where's Zammis?"

"Who?"

"Jeriba Zammis; the Drac that I was with."

The doctor shrugged. "I don't know anything about it, but I suppose the Draggers are taking care of it."

Draggers. I'd once used the term myself. As I listened to it coming out of Steerman's mouth, it seemed foreign: alien, repulsive. "Zammis is a Drac, not a Dragger."

The doctor's brows furrowed, then he shrugged. "Of course. Whatever you say. Just you get some rest, and I'll check back on you in a few hours."

"May I see Zammis?"

The doctor smiled. "Dear, no. You're on your way back to the Delphi USEB. The . . . Drac is probably on its way to Draco." He nodded, then turned and left. God, I felt lost. I looked around and saw that I was in the ward of a ship's sick bay. The beds on either side of me were occupied. The man on my right shook his head and went back to reading a magazine. The one on my left looked angry.

"You damned Dragger suck!" He turned on his left side and presented me his back.

Alien Earth. As I stepped down the ramp onto the USE field in Orleans, those were the first two words that popped into my head. Alien Earth. I looked at the crowds of USE Force personnel bustling around like so many ants, inhaled the smell of industrial man, then spat on the ramp.

"How you like, put in stockade time?"

I looked down and saw a white-capped Force Police private glaring up at me. I continued down the ramp. "Get bent."

"*Quoi?*" The FP marched over and met me at the end of the ramp.

"Get bent." I pulled my discharge papers from my breast pocket and waved them. "*Gavey* shorttimer, *kizlode?"*

The FP took my papers, frowned at them, then pointed at a long, low building at the edge of the field. *"Continuez tout droit."*

I smiled, turned and headed across the field, thinking of Zammis asking about how humans talk together. And where was Zammis? I shook my head, then entered the building. Most of the people inside the low building were crowding the in-processing or transportation-exchange aisles. I saw two bored officials behind two long tables and figured that they were the local customs clerks. A multilingual sign above their stations confirmed the hunch. I stopped in front of one of them. She glanced up at me, then held out her hand. *"Vôtre passeport?"*

I pulled out the blue and white booklet, handed it over, then stood holding my hands as I waited. I could feel the muscles at the back of my neck knot as I observed an old anti-Drac propaganda poster on the wall behind her. It showed two yellow, clawed hands holding a miniature Earth before a fanged mouth. Fangs and claws. The caption read: "They would call this victory" in seven languages.

"Avez-vous quelque chose à déclarer?"

I frowned at her. *"Ess?"*

She frowned back. *"Avez-vous quelque chose à déclarer?"*

I felt a tap on my back. "Do you speak English?"

I turned and saw the other customs clerk. My upper lip curled. *"Surda; ne surda. Adze Dracon?"*

His eyebrows went up as he mouthed the word "Drac." He turned to the other clerk, took my passport from her, then looked back at me. He tapped the booklet against his fingertips, then opened it, read the ident page, and looked back at me. "Come with me, Mister Davidge. We must have a talk." He turned and headed into a small office. I shrugged and followed. When I entered, he pointed toward a chair. As I lowered myself into it, he sat down behind a desk. "Why do you pretend not to speak English?"

"Why do you have that poster on the wall? The war is over."

The customs clerk clasped his hands, rested them on the desk, then shook his head. "The fighting is over, Mister Davidge, but for many the war is not. The Draggers killed many humans."

I cocked my head to one side. "A few Dracs died, too." I stood up. "May I go now?"

The customs clerk leaned back in his chair. "That chip on your shoulder you will find to be a considerable weight to bear on this planet."

"I'm the one who has to carry it."

The customs clerk shrugged, then nodded toward the door. "You may go. And good luck, Mister Davidge. You'll need it."

"Dragger suck." As an invective the term had all of the impact of several historical terms— Quisling, heretic, fag, nigger-lover, all rolled into one. Ex-Force pilots were a drag on the employment market, with no commercial positions open, especially not to a pilot who hadn't flown in four years, who had a gimpy leg, and who was a Dragger suck. Transportation to North America, and after a period of lonely wandering, to Dallas. Mistan's eight-hundred-year-old words from the *Talman* would haunt me: *Misnuuram va siddeth*; Your thought is loneliness. Loneliness is a thing one does to oneself. *Jerry shook his head that one time, then pointed a yellow finger at me as the words it wanted to say came together. "Davidge . . . to me loneliness is a discomfort—unpleasant, and a thing to be avoided, but not a thing to be feared. I think you would prefer death to being alone with yourself."*

Mistan observed: "If you are alone with yourself, you will forever be alone with others." A contradiction? The test of reality proves it true. I was out of place on my own planet, and it was more than a hate that I didn't share or a love that, to others, seemed impossible—perverse. Deep inside of myself, I had no use for the creature called "Davidge." Before Fyrine IV there had been other reasons—reasons that I could not identify; but now, my reason was known. My fault or not, I had betrayed an ugly, yellow thing called Zammis, as well as the creature's parent. *"Present Zammis before the Jeriba archives. Swear this to me."*

Oh, Jerry . . .
Swear this!
I swear it . . .

I had forty-eight thousand credits in back pay, and so money wasn't a problem. The problem was what to do with myself. Finally, in Dallas, I landed a job in a small book house translating manuscripts into Drac. It seemed that there was a craving among Dracs for Westerns: "Stick 'em up *naagusaat!*"

"*Nu geph*, lawman." Thang, thang! The guns flashed and another *kizlode shaddsaat* bit the dust.

I quit.

I finally called my parents. *Why didn't you call before, Willy? We've been worried sick . . . Had a few*

*things I had to straighten out, Dad . . . No, not really
. . . Well, we understand, son . . . It must have
been awful . . . Dad, I'd like to come home for a
while . . .*

Even before I put down the money on the used
Dearman Electric, I knew I was making a mistake
going home. I felt the need of a home, but the one I
had left at the age of eighteen wasn't it. But I
headed there because there was nowhere else to
go.

I drove alone in the dark, using only the old
roads, the quiet hum of the Dearman's motor the
only sound. The December midnight was clear,
and I could see the stars through the car's bubble
canopy. Fyrine IV drifted into my thoughts, the
raging ocean, the endless winds. I pulled off the
road onto the shoulder and killed the lights. In a
few minutes, my eyes adjusted to the dark and I
stepped outside and shut the door. Kansas has a
big sky, and the stars seemed close enough to
touch. Snow crunched under my feet as I looked
up, trying to pick Fyrine out of the thousands of
visible stars.

Fyrine is in the constellation Pegasus, but my
eyes were not practiced enough to pick the winged
horse out from the surrounding stars. I shrugged,
felt a chill, and decided to get back in the car. As I
put my hand on the doorlatch, I saw a constellation that I did recognize, north, hanging just above
the horizon: Draco. The Dragon, its tail twisted
around Ursa Minor, hung upside down in the sky.
Eltanin, the Dragon's nose, is the homestar of the
Dracs. Its second planet, Draco, was Zammis's
home.

Headlights from an approaching car blinded me,
and I turned toward the car as it pulled to a stop.
The window on the driver's side opened and some-

one spoke from the darkness.

"You need some help?"

I shook my head. "No, thank you." I held up a hand. "I was just looking at the stars."

"Quite a night, isn't it?"

"Sure is."

"Sure you don't need any help?"

I shook my head. "Thanks . . . wait. Where is the nearest commercial spaceport?"

"About an hour ahead in Salina."

"Thanks." I saw a hand wave from the window, then the other car pulled away. I took another look at Eltanin, then got back in my car.

Nine weeks later I stood before the little gray man who ran Lone Star Publishing, Inc. He looked up at me and frowned. "So, what do you want? I thought you quit."

I threw a thousand-page manuscript on his desk. "This."

He poked it with a finger. "What is it?"

"The Drac bible; it's called the *Talman*."

"So what?"

"So it's the only book tanslated from Drac into English; so it's the explanation for how every Drac conducts itself; so it'll make you a bundle of credits."

He leaned forward, scanned several pages, then looked up at me. "You know, Davidge, I don't like you worth a damn."

I shrugged. "I don't like you either."

He returned to the manuscript. "Why now?"

"Now is when I need money."

He shrugged. "The best I can offer would be around eight or ten thousand. This is untried stuff."

"I need twenty-four thousand. You want to go for less than that, I'll take it to someone else."

He looked at me and frowned. "What makes you think anyone else would be interested?"

"Let's quit playing around. There are a lot of survivors of the war—both military and civilian—who would like to understand what happened." I leaned forward and tapped the manuscript. "That's what's in there."

"Twenty-four thousand is lot for a first manuscript."

I gathered up the pages. "I'll find someone who has some coin to invest in a sure thing."

He placed his hand on the manuscript. "Hold on, Davidge." He frowned. "Twenty-four thousand?"

"Not a quarter-note less."

He pursed his lips, then glanced at me. "I suppose you'll be Hell on wheels regarding final approval."

I shook my head. "All I want is the money. You can do whatever you want with the manuscript."

He leaned back in his chair, looked at the manuscript, then back at me. "The money. What're you going to do with it?"

"None of your business."

He leaned forward, then leafed through a few more pages. His eyebrows notched up, then he looked back at me. "You aren't picky about the contract?"

"As long as I get the money, you can turn that into *Mein Kampf* if you want to."

He leafed through a few more pages. "This is some pretty radical stuff."

"It sure is. And you can find the same stuff in Plato, Aristotle, Augustine, James, Freud,

Szasz, Nortmyer, and the Declaration of Independence."

He leaned back in his chair. "What does this mean to you?"

"Twenty-four thousand credits."

He leafed through a few more pages, then a few more. In twelve hours I had purchased passage to Draco.

Six months later, I stood in front of an ancient cut-stone gate wondering what in the hell I was doing. The trip to Draco, with nothing but Dracs as companions on the last leg, showed me the truth in Namvaac's words "Peace is often only war without fighting." The accords, on paper, gave me the right to travel to the planet, but the Drac bureaucrats and their paperwork wizards had perfected the big stall long before the first human step into space. It took threats, bribes, and long days of filling out forms, being checked and rechecked for disease, contraband, reason for visit, filling out more forms, refilling out the forms I had already filled out, more bribes, waiting, waiting, waiting . . .

On the ship, I spent most of my time in my cabin, but since the Drac stewards refused to serve me, I went to the ship's lounge for my meals. I sat alone, listening to the comments about me from other booths. I had figured the path of least resistance was to pretend I didn't understand what they were saying. It is always assumed that humans do not speak Drac.

"Must we eat in the same compartment with the *Irkmaan* slime?"

"Look at it, how its pale skin blotches—and that

evil-smelling thatch on top. Feh! The smell!"

I ground my teeth a little and kept my glance riveted to my plate.

"It defies the *Talman* that the universe's laws could be so corrupt as to produce a creature such as that."

I turned and faced the three Dracs sitting in the booth across the aisle from mine. In Drac, I replied: "If your line's elders had seen fit to teach the village *kiz* to use contraceptives, you wouldn't even exist." I returned to my food while the two Dracs struggled to hold the third Drac down.

On Draco, it was no problem finding the Jeriba estate. The problem was getting in. A high stone wall enclosed the property, and from the gate, I could see the huge stone mansion that Jerry had described to me. I told the guard at the gate that I wanted to see Jeriba Zammis. The guard stared at me, then went into an alcove behind the gate. In a few moments, another Drac emerged from the mansion and walked quickly across the wide lawn to the gate. The Drac nodded at the guard, then stopped and faced me. It was a dead ringer for Jerry.

"You are the *Irkmaan* that asked to see Jeriba Zammis?"

I nodded. "Zammis must have told you about me. I'm Willis Davidge."

The Drac studied me. "I am Estone Nev, Jeriba Shigan's sibling. My parent, Jeriba Gothig, wishes to see you." The Drac turned abruptly and walked back to the mansion. I followed, feeling heady at the thought of seeing Zammis again. I paid little attention to my surroundings until I was ushered into a large room with a vaulted stone ceiling. Jerry had told me that the house was four thousand years old. I believed it. As I entered, another Drac stood and walked over to me. It was old, but I knew who it was.

"You are Gothig, Shigan's parent."

The yellow eyes studied me. "Who are you, *Irkmaan?*" It held out a wrinkled, three-fingered hand. "What do you know of Jeriba Zammis, and why do you speak the Drac tongue with the style and accent of my child Shigan? What are you here for?"

"I speak Drac in this manner because that is the way Jeriba Shigan taught me to speak it."

The old Drac cocked its head to one side and narrowed its yellow eyes. "You knew my child? How?"

"Didn't the survey commission tell you?"

"It was reported to me that my child, Shigan, was killed in the battle of Fyrine IV. That was over six of our years ago. What is your game, *Irkmaan?*"

I turned from Gothig to Nev. The younger Drac was examining me with the same look of suspicion. I turned back to Gothig. "Shigan wasn't killed in the battle. We were stranded together on the surface of Fyrine IV and lived there for a year. Shigan died giving birth to Jeriba Zammis. A year later the joint survey commission found us and—"

"Enough! Enough of this, *Irkmaan!* Are you here for money, to use my influence for trade concessions—what?"

I frowned. "Where is Zammis?"

Tears of anger came to the old Drac's eyes.

"There is no Zammis, *Irkmaan!* The Jeriba line ended with the death of Shigan!"

My eyes grew wide as I shook my head. "That's not true. I know. I took care of Zammis—you heard nothing from the commission?"

"Get to the point of your scheme, *Irkmaan.* I haven't all day."

I studied Gothig. The old Drac had heard nothing from the commission. The Drac authorities took Zammis, and the child had evaporated. Gothig had been told nothing. Why? "I was with Shigan, Gothig. That is how I learned your language. When Shigan died giving birth to Zammis, I—"

"*Irkmaan*, if you cannot get to your scheme, I will have to ask Nev to throw you out. Shigan died in the battle of Fyrine IV. The Drac Fleet notified us only days later."

I nodded. "Then, Gothig, tell me how I came to know the line of Jeriba? Do you wish me to recite it for you?"

Gothig snorted. "You say you know the Jeriba line?"

"Yes."

Gothig flipped a hand at me. "Then, recite."

I took a breath, then began. By the time I had reached the hundred and seventy-third generation, Gothig had knelt on the stone floor next to Nev. The Dracs remained that way for three hours of the recital. When I concluded, Gothig bowed its head and wept. "Yes, *Irkmaan*, yes. You must have known Shigan. Yes." The old Drac looked up into my face, its eyes wide with hope. "And, you say Shigan continued the line—that Zammis was born?"

I nodded. "I don't know why the commission didn't notify you."

Gothig got to its feet and frowned. "We will find out, *Irkmaan*—what is your name?"

"Davidge. Willis Davidge."

"We will find out, Davidge."

Gothig arranged quarters for me in its house, which was fortunate, since I had little more than eleven hundred credits left. After making a host of inquiries, Gothig sent Nev and me to the Chamber Center in Sendievu, Draco's capital city. The Jeriba line, I found, was influential, and the big stall was held down to a minimum. Eventually, we were directed to the Joint Survey Commission representative, a Drac named Jozzdn Vrule. It looked up from the letter Gothig had given me and frowned. "Where did you get this, *Irkmaan*?"

"I believe the signature is on it."

The Drac looked at the paper, then back at me. "The Jeriba line is one of the most respected on Draco. You say that Jeriba Gothig gave you this?"

"I felt certain I said that; I could feel my lips moving—"

Nev stepped in. "You have the dates and the information concerning the Fyrine IV survey mission. We want to know what happened to Jeriba Zammis."

Jozzdn Vrule frowned and looked back at the paper. "Estone Nev, you are the founder of your line, is this not true?"

"It is true."

"Would you found your line in shame? Why do I see you with this *Irkmaan*?"

Nev curled its upper lip and folded its arms.

"Jozzdn Vrule, if you contemplate walking this planet in the foreseeable future as a free being, it would be to your profit to stop working your mouth and to start finding Jeriba Zammis."

Jozzdn Vrule looked down and studied its fingers, then returned its glance to Nev. "Very well, Estone Nev. You threaten me if I fail to hand you the truth. I think you will find the truth the greater threat." The Drac scribbled on a piece of paper, then handed it to Nev. "You will find Jeriba Zammis at this address, and you will curse the day that I gave you this."

We entered the retard colony feeling sick. All around us, Dracs stared with vacant eyes, or screamed, or foamed at the mouth, or behaved as lower-order creatures. After we had arrived, Gothig joined us. The Drac director of the colony frowned at me and shook its head at Gothig. "Turn back now, while it is still possible, Jeriba Gothig. Beyond this room lies nothing but pain and sorrow."

Gothig grabbed the director by the front of its wraps. "Hear me, insect: If Jeriba Zammis is within these walls, bring my grandchild forth! Else, I shall bring the might of the Jeriba line down upon your pointed head!"

The director lifted its head, twitched its lips, then nodded. "Very well. Very well, you pompous *Kazzmidth*! We tried to protect the Jeriba reputation. We tried! But now you shall see." The director nodded and pursed its lips. "Yes, you overwealthy fashion follower, now you shall see." The director scribbled on a piece of paper, then

but take it! Yes, take it! See this being you call
Jeriba Zammis. See it, and weep!"

Among trees and grass, Jeriba Zammis sat upon
a stone bench, staring at the ground. Its eyes never
blinked, its hands never moved. Gothig frowned at
me, but I could spare nothing for Shigan's parent. I
walked to Zammis. "Zammis, do you know me?"

The Drac retrieved its thoughts from a million
warrens and raised its yellow eyes to me. I saw no
sign of recognition. "Who are you?"

I squatted down, placed my hands on its arms
and shook them. "Dammit, Zammis, don't you
know me? I'm your uncle. Remember that? Uncle
Davidge?"

The Drac weaved on the bench, then shook its
head. It lifted an arm and waved to an orderly. "I
want to go to my room. Please, let me go to my
room."

I stood and grabbed Zammis by the front of its
hospital gown. "Zammis, it's me!"

The yellow eyes, dull and lifeless, stared back at
me. The orderly placed a yellow hand upon my
shoulder. "Let it go, *Irkmaan*."

"Zammis!" I turned to Nev and Gothig. "Say
something!"

The Drac orderly pulled a sap from its pocket,
then slapped it suggestively against the palm of its
hand. "Let it go, *Irkmaan*."

Gothig stepped forward. "Explain this!"

The orderly looked at Gothig, Nev, me, and then
Zammis. "This one—this creature—came to us
professing a love, a *love*, mind you, of humans! This

is no small perversion, Jeriba Gothig. The government would protect you from this scandal. Would you wish the line of Jeriba dragged into this?"

I looked at Zammis. "What have you done to Zammis, you *kizlode* sonofabitch? A little shock? A little drug? Rot out its mind?"

The orderly sneered at me, then shook his head. "You, *Irkmaan*, do not understand. This one would not be happy as an *Irkmaan vul*—a human lover. We are making it possible for this one to function in Drac society. You think this is wrong?"

I looked at Zammis and shook my head. I remembered too well my treatment at the hands of my fellow humans. "No. I don't think it's wrong . . . I just don't know."

The orderly turned to Gothig. "Please understand, Jeriba Gothig. We could not subject the Jeriba line to this disgrace. Your grandchild is almost well and will soon enter a reeducation program. In no more than two years, you will have a grandchild worthy of carrying on the Jeriba line. Is this wrong?"

Gothig only shook its head. I squatted down in front of Zammis and looked up into its yellow eyes. I reached up and took its right hand in both of mine. "Zammis?"

Zammis looked down, moved its left hand over, and picked up my left hand and spread the fingers. One at a time Zammis pointed at the fingers of my hand, then it looked into my eyes, then examined the hand again. "Yes . . ." Zammis pointed again. "One, two, three, *four, five!*" Zammis looked into my eyes. "Four, five!"

I nodded. "Yes. Yes."

Zammis pulled my hand to its cheek and held it

close. "Uncle . . . Uncle. I told you I'd never forget you."

I never counted the years that passed. Mistaan had words for those who count time as though their recognition of its passing marked their place in the Universe. Mornings, the weather as clear as weather gets on Fyrine IV, I would visit my friend's grave. Next to it, Estone Nev, Zammis, Ty and I buried Gothig. Shigan's parent had taken the healing Zammis, liquidated the Jeriba line's estate, then moved the whole shebang to Fyrine IV. When told the story, it was Ty who named the planet "Friendship."

One blustery day I knelt between the graves, replaced some rocks, then added a few more. I pulled my snakeskins tight against the wind, then sat down and looked out to sea. Still the rollers steamed in under the grey-black cover of clouds. Soon the ice would come. I looked at my scarred, wrinkled hands, then at the grave.

"I couldn't stay in the colony with them, Jerry. Don't get me wrong; it's nice. Damned nice. But I kept looking out my window, seeing the ocean, thinking of the cave. I'm alone, in a way. But it's good. I know what and who I am, Jerry, and that's all there is to it, right?"

I heard a noise. I crouched over, placed my hands upon my withered knees, and pushed myself to my feet. The Drac was coming from the colony compound, a child in its arms.

I rubbed my beard. "Eh, Ty, so that is your first child?"

The Drac nodded. "I would be pleased, Uncle, if

you would teach it what it must be taught: the line, the *Talman*; and about the life on Friendship."

I took the bundle into my arms. Chubby three-fingered arms waved at the air, then grasped my snakeskins. "Yes, Ty, this one is a Jeriba." I looked up at Ty. "And how is your parent, Zammis?"

Ty shrugged. "It is as well as can be expected. My parent wishes you well."

I nodded. "And the same to it, Ty. Zammis ought to get out of that air-conditioned capsule and come back to live in the cave. It'll do it good."

Ty grinned and nodded its head. "I will tell my parent, Uncle."

I stabbed my thumb into my chest. "Look at me! You don't see me sick, do you?"

"No, Uncle."

"You tell Zammis to kick that doctor out of there and to come back to the cave, hear?"

"Yes, Uncle." Ty smiled. "Is there anything you need?"

I nodded and scratched the back of my neck. "Toilet paper. Just a couple of packs. Maybe a couple of bottles of whiskey—no, forget the whiskey. I'll wait until Haesni, here, puts in its first year. Just the toilet paper."

Ty bowed. "Yes, Uncle, and may the many mornings find you well."

I waved my hand impatiently. "They will, they will. Just don't forget the toilet paper."

Ty bowed again. "I won't, Uncle."

Ty turned and walked through the scrub forest back to the colony. I lived with them for a year, but I moved out and went back to the cave. I gathered the wood, smoked the snake, and withstood the winter. Zammis gave me the young Ty to rear in the cave and now Ty had handed me Haesni. I nodded at the child. "Your child will be called Gothig, and then . . ." I looked at the sky and felt the tears drying on my face. ". . . and then, Gothig's child will be called Shigan." I nodded and headed for the cleft that would bring us down to the level of the cave.

0-595-30976-3

CPSIA information can be obtained at www.ICGtesting.com
Printed in the USA
LVOW08s0228101214

418100LV00001B/6/P